DATE DUE			

201-9500   PRINTED IN U.S.A.

FIREBIRD
WHERE FANTASY TAKES FLIGHT™

OTORI
CLAN

MARUYAMA
CLAN

SEISHUU
CLAN

SHIRAKAWA
CLAN

TOHAN
CLAN

TALES OF THE OTORI

EPISODE 2

Grass for His Pillow

THE WAY THROUGH THE SNOW

LIAN HEARN

FIREBIRD

AN IMPRINT OF PENGUIN GROUP (USA) INC.

FIREBIRD

Published by the Penguin Group

Penguin Group (USA) Inc., 345 Hudson Street, New York, New York 10014, U.S.A.

Penguin Group (Canada), 10 Alcorn Avenue, Toronto, Ontario, Canada M4V 3B2
(a division of Pearson Penguin Canada Inc.)

Registered Offices: Penguin Books Ltd, 80 Strand, London WC2R 0RL, England

This is a work of fiction. Names, characters, places, and incidents either are the product of the
author's imagination or are used fictitiously, and any resemblance to actual persons, living or dead,
business establishments, events, or locales is entirely coincidental.

The author gratefully acknowledges permission to quote from *From the Country of Eight Islands*
by Hiroaki Sato, translated by Burton Watson. Used by permission of Doubleday,
a division of Random House, Inc.

Excerpt from "Kinuta" from *Japanese Noh Drama*, edited by Royall Tyler, Penguin Classics.

First published in the United States of America by Riverhead Books,
a member of Penguin Group (USA) Inc., 2003
Published by Firebird, an imprint of Penguin Group (USA) Inc., 2005

1 3 5 7 9 10 8 6 4 2

THE LIBRARY OF CONGRESS HAS CATALOGUED THE RIVERHEAD EDITION AS FOLLOWS:
Hearn, Lian.
Grass for his pillow / Lian Hearn.
p.   cm.—(Tales of the Otori ; bk. 2)
Sequel to: Across the nightingale floor.
ISBN 1-57322-251-8
1. Teenage boys—Fiction. 2. Orphans—Fiction. 3. Japan—Fiction. I. Title.
PR9619.3.H3725G73 2003   2003043215
823'.914—dc21

ISBN 0-14-240432-2

Printed in China

To D.

FOREWORD

These events took place in the year following the death of Otori Shigeru in the Tohan stronghold of Inuyama. The leader of the Tohan clan, Iida Sadamu, was killed in revenge by Shigeru's adopted son, Otori Takeo, or so it was widely believed, and the Tohan overthrown by Arai Daiichi, one of the Seishuu clan from Kumamoto, who took advantage of the chaos following the fall of Inuyama to seize control of the Three Countries. Arai had hoped to form an alliance with Takeo and arrange his marriage to Shirakawa Kaede, now the heir to the Maruyama and Shirakawa domains.

However, torn between Shigeru's last commands and the demands of his real father's family, the Kikuta of the Tribe, Takeo gave up his inheritance and marriage with Kaede, with whom he was deeply in love, to go with the Tribe, feeling himself bound to them by blood and by oath.

Otori Shigeru was buried at Terayama, a remote mountain temple in the heart of the Middle Country. After the battles of Inuyama and Kushimoto, Arai visited the temple to pay his respects to his fallen ally and to confirm the new alliances. Here Takeo and Kaede met for the last time.

THE THREE COUNTRIES

------- fief boundaries

.... fief boundaries
before Yaegahara

- - - - - high road

battlefields

castletown

shrine

temple

CHARACTERS

The Clans

THE OTORI
(Middle Country; castle town: Hagi)

Otori Shigeru: rightful heir to the clan

Otori Takeshi: his younger brother, murdered by the Tohan clan **(d.)**

Otori Takeo: (born Tomasu) his adopted son

Otori Shigemori: Shigeru's father, killed at the battle of Yaegahara **(d.)**

Otori Ichiro: a distant relative, Shigeru and Takeo's teacher

Chiyo

Haruka: maids in the household

Shiro: a carpenter

Otori Shoichi: Shigeru's uncle, now lord of the clan

Otori Masahiro: Shoichi's younger brother

Otori Yoshitomi: Masahiro's son

Miyoshi Kahei: brothers, friends of Takeo
Miyoshi Gemba

Miyoshi Satoru: their father, captain of the guard in Hagi castle

Endo Chikara: a senior retainer

Terada Fumifusa: a pirate
Terada Fumio: his son, friend of Takeo

Ryoma: a fisherman, Masahiro's illegitimate son

THE TOHAN
(The East; castle town: Inuyama)

Iida Sadamu: lord of the clan
Iida Nariaki: Sadamu's cousin

Ando, Abe: Iida's retainers

Lord Noguchi: an ally
Lady Noguchi: his wife
Junko: a servant in Noguchi castle

THE SEISHUU
*(An alliance of several ancient families in the West;
main castle towns: Kumamoto and Maruyama)*

Arai Daiichi: a warlord

Niwa Satoru: a retainer
Akita Tsutomu: a retainer
Sonoda Mitsuru: Akita's nephew
Maruyama Naomi: head of the Maruyama domain,
    Shigeru's lover

Mariko: her daughter
Sachie: her maid

Sugita Haruki: a retainer
Sugita Hiroshi: his nephew
Sakai Masaki: Hiroshi's cousin

Lord Shirakawa
Kaede: Shirakawa's eldest daughter, Lady Maruyama's cousin
Ai, Hana: Shirakawa's daughters

Ayame
Manami
Akane: maids in the household

Amano Tenzo: a Shirakawa retainer

Shoji Kiyoshi: senior retainer to Lord Shirakawa

The Tribe

THE MUTO FAMILY

Muto Kenji: Takeo's teacher, the master
Muto Shizuka: Kenji's niece, Arai's mistress, and Kaede's
    companion
Zenko, Taku: her sons
Muto Seiko: Kenji's wife
Muto Yuki: their daughter
Muto Yuzuru: a cousin

Kana
Miyabi: maids

THE KIKUTA FAMILY

Kikuta Isamu: Takeo's real father (d.)
Kikuta Kotaro: his cousin, the Master
Kikuta Gosaburo: Kotaro's younger brother
Kikuta Akio: their nephew
Kikuta Hajime: a wrestler
Sadako: a maid

THE KURODA FAMILY

Kuroda Shintaro: a famous assassin
Kondo Kiichi
Imai Kazuo
Kudo Keiko

Others

Lord Fujiwara: a nobleman, exiled from the capital
Mamoru: his protégé and companion
Ono Rieko: his cousin
Murita: a retainer

Matsuda Shingen: the abbot at Terayama
Kubo Makoto: a monk, Takeo's closest friend

Jin-emon: a bandit

Jiro: a farmer's son

Jo-An: an outcast

Horses

Raku: gray with black mane and tail, Takeo's first horse, given
    by him to Kaede
Kyu: black, Shigeru's horse, disappeared in Inuyama
Aoi: black, half brother to Kyu
Ki: Amano's chestnut
Shun: Takeo's bay, a very clever horse

bold = main characters

(d.) = character died before the start of *Across the Nightingale Floor,*
    Episode 1

貧窮問答の歌　一首

風雑へ　雨降る夜の　雨雑へ
雪降る夜は　術もなく　寒くし
あれば　堅塩を　取りつづしろひ
糟湯酒　うち啜ろひて　咳かひ
鼻びしびしに　しかとあらぬ　髭
かき撫でて　我を除きて　人はあらじと
誇ろへど　寒くしあれば　麻衾
引き被り　布肩衣　有りのことごと
服襲へども　寒き夜すらを　我
よりも　貧しき人の　父母は　飢え
寒ゆらむ

……後略……

「万葉集」巻五
八九二

On nights when, wind mixing in, the rain falls,

On nights when, rain mixing in, the snow falls

YAMANOUE NO OKURA:
A DIALOGUE ON POVERTY.
FROM *THE COUNTRY OF THE EIGHT
ISLANDS*
TRANS: HIROAKI SATO

Grass for His Pillow

THE WAY THROUGH THE SNOW

·1·

Matsue was a northern town, cold and austere. We arrived in the middle of autumn, when the wind from the mainland howled across a sea as dark as iron. Once the snows began, like Hagi, Matsue would be cut off from the rest of the country for three months. It was as good a place as any to learn what I had to learn.

For a week we had walked all day, following the coastal road. It did not rain, but the sky was often overcast and each day was shorter and colder than the last. We stopped at many villages and showed the children juggling, spinning tops, and games with string that Yuki and Keiko knew. At night we always found shelter with merchants who were part of the

Tribe network. I lay awake till late listening to whispered conversations, my nostrils filled with the smells of the brewery or of soybean foodstuff. I dreamed of Kaede, and longed for her, and sometimes when I was alone I would take out Shigeru's letter and read his last words, in which he had charged me to avenge his death and to take care of Lady Shirakawa. Consciously I had made the decision to go to the Tribe, but, even in those early days, just before sleep, unbidden images came to me of his uncles, unpunished in Hagi, and of his sword, Jato, sleeping at Terayama.

By the time we arrived at Matsue, Yuki and I were lovers. It happened with inevitability, yet not through my will. I was always aware of her on the road, my senses tuned to her voice, her scent. But I was too unsure of my future, my position in the group, too guarded and wary to make any move toward her. It was obvious that Akio also found her attractive. He was at ease with her as with no one else, seeking out her company, walking beside her on the road, sitting next to her at meals. I did not want to antagonize him further.

Yuki's position in the group was unclear. She deferred to Akio and always treated him with respect; yet, she seemed equal to him in status and, as I had reason to know, her skills were greater. Keiko was obviously lower down in the order, perhaps from a lesser family or a collateral branch. She continued to ignore me, but showed blind loyalty to Akio. As for the older man, Kazuo, everyone treated him as a mixture between a servant and an uncle. He had many practical skills, including thievery.

Akio was Kikuta through both father and mother. He was a second cousin to me and had the same hands shaped like mine. His physical skills were astounding—he had the fastest reflexes of anyone I've ever met, and could leap so high he seemed to be flying—but apart from his ability to perceive the use of invisibility and the second self, and his dexterity in juggling, none of the more unusual Kikuta gifts had come to him. Yuki told me this one day when we were walking some way ahead of the others.

"The masters fear the gifts are dying out. Every generation seems to have fewer." She gave me a sideways look and added, "That's why it's so important to us to keep you."

Her mother had said the same thing and I would have liked to have heard more, but Akio shouted at me that it was my turn to push the cart. I saw the jealousy in his face as I walked toward him. I understood it and his hostility to me all too well. He was fanatically loyal to the Tribe, having been raised in their teachings and way of life; I could not help but realize that my sudden appearance was likely to usurp many of his ambitions and hopes. But understanding his antipathy did not make it any easier to bear, nor did it make me like him.

I said nothing as I took the handles of the cart from him. He ran forward to walk beside Yuki, whispering to her, forgetting, as he often did, that I could hear every word. He'd taken to calling me the Dog, and the nickname had enough truth in it to stick. As I've said before, I have an affinity with dogs: I can hear the things they hear, and I've known what it's like to be speechless.

"What were you saying to the Dog?" he asked her.

"Teaching, teaching," she replied offhandedly. "There's so much he needs to learn."

But what she turned out to be best at teaching was the art of love.

Both Yuki and Keiko took on the role of prostitutes on the road if they needed to. So did many of the Tribe, men and women, no one thinking any the worse of them for it. It was simply another role to assume, then discard. Of course, the clans had quite different ideas about the virginity of their brides and the fidelity of their wives. Men could do what they liked; women were expected to be chaste. The teachings I had grown up with were somewhere between the two: The Hidden are supposed to be pure in matters of physical desire, but in practice are forgiving of one another's lapses, as they are in all things.

On our fourth night we stayed in a large village with a wealthy family. Despite the scarcity in the whole area following the storms, they had stockpiles of supplies and they were generous hosts. The merchant offered us women, maids from his household, and Akio and Kazuo accepted. I made an excuse of some sort, which brought a storm of teasing, but the matter was not forced. Later, when the girls came to the room and lay down with the other men, I moved my mattress outside onto the veranda and shivered under the brittle ice points of the stars. Desire, longing for Kaede—to be honest, at that moment for any woman—tormented me. The door slid open, and one of the girls from the household, I thought, came out onto the veranda. As she closed the door behind her, I caught her fragrance and recognized her tread.

Yuki knelt beside me. I reached out for her and pulled her down next to me. Her girdle was already undone, her robe loose. I remember feeling the most immense gratitude to her. She loosened my clothes, making it all so easy for me—too easy; I was too quick. She scolded me for my impatience, promising to teach me. And so she did.

The next morning Akio looked at me searchingly. "You changed your mind last night?"

I wondered how he knew—if he had heard us through the flimsy screens or if he was just guessing.

"One of the girls came to me. It seemed impolite to turn her away," I replied.

He grunted and did not pursue the matter, but he watched Yuki and me carefully, even though we said nothing to each other, as though he knew something had changed between us. I thought about her constantly, swinging between elation and despair: elation because the act of love with her was indescribably wonderful; despair because she was not Kaede, and because what we did together bound me ever more closely to the Tribe.

I couldn't help remembering Kenji's comment as he left: *It's a good thing Yuki's going to be around to keep an eye on you.* He had known this would happen. Had he planned it with her, instructed her? Did Akio of course know, because he had been told? I was filled with misgivings, and I did not trust Yuki, but it didn't stop me from going to her every time I had the chance. She, so much wiser in these matters, made sure the chance arose often. And Akio's jealousy grew more apparent every day.

So our little group came to Matsue, outwardly united and in harmony, but in fact torn by intense emotions that, being true members of the Tribe, we concealed from outsiders and from one another.

We stayed at the Kikuta house, another merchant's place, smelling of fermenting soybeans, paste, and sauce. The owner, Gosaburo, was Kotaro's youngest brother, also first cousin to my father. There was little need for secrecy. We were now well beyond the Three Countries and Arai's reach, and in Matsue the local clan, the Yoshida, had no quarrel with the Tribe, finding them equally useful for moneylending, spying, and assassination. Here we had news of Arai, who was busy subduing the East and the Middle Country, making alliances, fighting border skirmishes, and setting up his administration. We heard the first rumors of his campaign against the Tribe and his intention to clear his lands of them, rumors that were the source of much mirth and derision.

I will not set down the details of my training. Its aim was to harden my heart and instill in me ruthlessness. But even now, years later, the memory of its harshness and cruelty makes me flinch and want to turn my eyes away. They were cruel times: Maybe Heaven was angry, maybe men were taken over by devils, maybe when the powers of good weaken, the brutal, with its nose for rot, storms in. The Tribe, cruelest of the cruel, flourished.

I was not the only Tribe member in training. There were several other boys, most of them much younger, all of them born Kikuta and raised in the family. The one closest to me in age was a solidly built, cheerful-faced young man with whom I was often paired. His name was Hajime, and though he did not exactly deflect Akio's rage toward me—to do so openly would be unthinkably disobedient—he often managed to draw some of it away. There was something about him I liked, though I would not go as far as to say I trusted him. His fighting skills were far greater than mine. He was a wrestler, and also strong enough to pull the huge bows of the master archers, but in the skills that are given rather than learned, neither he nor any of the others came near what I could do. It was only now that I began to realize how exceptional these skills were. I could go invisible for minutes on end, even in the bare white-walled hall; sometimes not even Akio could see me. I could split myself while fighting and watch my opponent grapple with my second self from the other side of the room. I could move without sound while my own hearing became ever more acute, and the younger boys quickly learned never to look me directly in the eye. I had put all of them to sleep at one time or another. I was learning slowly to control this skill as I practiced on them. When I looked into their eyes I saw the weaknesses and fears that made them vulnerable to my gaze: sometimes their own inner fears, sometimes fear of me and the uncanny powers that had been given to me.

Every morning I did exercises with Akio to build up strength and speed. I was slower and weaker than he was in almost all areas, and he had gained nothing in patience. But to give him his due, he was determined to teach me some of his skills in leaping and flying, and he succeeded. Part of those skills were in me already—my stepfather, after all, used to call me a wild monkey—and Akio's brutal but skillful teaching drew them to the surface and showed me how to control them. After only a few weeks I was aware of the difference in me, of how much I had hardened in mind and body.

We always finished with fighting bare-handed—not that the Tribe used this art much, preferring assassination to actual combat—but we were all trained in it. Then we sat in silent meditation, a robe slung across our cooling bodies, keeping our body temperature up by force of will. My head was usually ringing from some blow or fall, and I did not empty my mind as I was supposed to but instead dwelt savagely on how I would like to see Akio suffer. I gave to him all of Jo-An's torment that he'd once described to me.

My training was designed to encourage cruelty, and I embraced it at the time wholeheartedly, glad for the skills it was giving me, delighted at how they enhanced those I had learned with the Otori warriors' sons back when Shigeru was still alive. My father's Kikuta blood came to life in me. My mother's compassion drained away, along with all the teachings of my childhood. I no longer prayed; neither the Secret God, nor the Enlightened One, nor the old spirits meant anything to me. I did not believe in their existence and I saw no evidence that they favored those who did. Sometimes in the night I would wake suddenly and catch an unprotected glimpse of myself, and shudder at what I was becoming, and then I would rise silently and, if I could, go and find Yuki, lie down with her, and lose myself in her.

We never spent the whole night together. Our encounters were always short and usually silent. But one afternoon we found ourselves alone in the house, apart from the servants who were occupied in the shop. Akio and Hajime had taken the younger boys to the shrine for some dedication ceremony, and I had been told to copy some documents for Gosaburo. I was grateful for the task. I rarely held a brush in my hands, and because I had learned to write so late, I was always afraid the characters would desert me. The merchant had a few books and, as Shigeru had instructed me, I read whenever I could, but I had lost my inkstone and brushes at Inuyama and had hardly written since.

I diligently copied the documents—records from the shop, accounts of the amount of soybeans and rice purchased from local farmers—but my fingers were itching to draw. I was reminded of my first visit to Terayama, the brilliance of the summer day, the beauty of the paintings, the little mountain bird I had drawn and given to Kaede.

As always, when I was thinking of the past, my heart unguarded, she came to me and took possession of me all over again. I could feel her presence, smell the fragrance of her hair, hear her voice. So strongly was she with me, I had a moment of fear, as if her ghost had slipped into the room. Her ghost would be angry with me, filled with resentment and rage for abandoning her. Her words rang in my ears: *I'm afraid of myself. I only feel safe with you.*

It was cold in the room and already growing dark, with all the threat of the winter to come. I shivered, full of remorse and regret. My hands were numb with cold.

I could hear Yuki's footsteps approaching from the back of the building. I started writing again. She crossed the courtyard and stepped out of her sandals onto the veranda of the records room. I could smell burning charcoal. She had brought a small brazier, which she placed on the floor next to me.

"You look cold," she said. "Shall I bring tea?"

"Later, maybe." I laid down the brush and held my hands out to the warmth. She took them and rubbed them between her own.

"I'll close the shutters," she said.

"Then you'll have to bring a lamp. I can't see to write."

She laughed quietly. The wooden shutters slid into place, one after another. The room went dim, lit only by the faint glow of the charcoal. When Yuki came back to me she had already loosened her robe. Soon we were both warm. But after the act of love, as wonderful as ever, my unease returned. Kaede's spirit had been in the room with me. Was I causing her anguish and arousing her jealousy and spite?

Curled against me, the heat radiating from her, Yuki said, "A message came from your cousin."

"Which cousin?" I had dozens of them now.

"Muto Shizuka."

I eased myself away from Yuki so she would not hear the quickened beating of my heart. "What did she say?"

"Lady Shirakawa is dying. Shizuka said she feared the end was very near." Yuki added in her indolent, sated voice, "Poor thing."

She was glowing with life and pleasure. But the only thing I was aware of in the room was Kaede, her frailty, her intensity, her supernatural beauty. I called out to her in my soul: *You cannot die. I must see you again. I will come for you. Don't die before I see you again!*

Her spirit gazed on me, her eyes dark with reproach and sorrow.

Yuki turned and looked up at me, surprised by my

silence. "Shizuka thought you should know: Was there something between you? My father hinted as much, but he said it was just green love. He said everyone who saw her became infatuated with her."

I did not answer. Yuki sat up, pulling her robe around her. "It was more than that, wasn't it? You loved her." She seized my hands and turned me to face her. "You loved her," she repeated, the jealousy beginning to show in her voice. "Is it over?"

"It will never be over," I said. "Even if she dies I can never stop loving her." Now that it was too late to tell Kaede, I knew that it was true.

"That part of your life is finished," Yuki said quietly but fiercely. "All of it. Forget her! You will never see her again." I could hear the anger and frustration in her voice.

"I would never have told you if you had not mentioned her." I pulled my hands away from her and dressed again. The warmth had gone from me as swiftly as it had come. The brazier was cooling.

"Bring some more charcoal," I told Yuki. "And lamps. I must finish the work."

"Takeo—" she began, and then broke off abruptly. "I'll

send the maid," she said, getting to her feet. She touched the back of my neck as she left, but I made no response. Physically we had been deeply involved: Her hands had massaged me, and struck me in punishment. We had killed side by side; we had made love. But she had barely brushed the surface of my heart, and at that moment we both knew it.

I made no sign of my grief, but I wept inwardly for Kaede and for the life that we might have had together. No further word came from Shizuka, though I never stopped listening for messengers. Yuki did not mention the subject again. I could not believe Kaede was dead, and in the daytime I clung to that belief, but the nights were different.

The last of the color faded as leaves fell from maple and willow. Strings of wild geese flew southward across the sullen sky. Messengers became less frequent as the town began to close down for winter. But they still came from time to time, bringing news of Tribe activities and of the fighting in the Three Countries, and, always, bringing new orders for our trade.

For that was how we described our work of spying and killing: trade, with human lives measured out as so many units. I copied records of these, too, often sitting till late into the night with Gosaburo, the merchant, moving from the soybean harvest to the other, deadlier one. Both showed a fine profit, though the soybeans had been affected by the storms while the murders had not, though one candidate for assassination had drowned before the Tribe could get to him and there was an ongoing dispute about payment.

The Kikuta, being more ruthless, were supposed to be more skilled at assassination than the Muto, who were traditionally the most effective spies. These two families were the aristocracy of the Tribe; the other three, Kuroda, Kudo, and Imai, worked at more menial and humdrum tasks, being servants, petty thieves, informants, and so on. Because the traditional skills were so valued, there were many marriages between Muto and Kikuta, fewer between them and the other families, though the exceptions often threw up geniuses like the assassin Shintaro.

After dealing with the accounts, Kikuta Gosaburo would give me lessons in genealogy, explaining the intricate relationships of the Tribe that spread like an autumn spider's web across the Three Countries, into the North and beyond. He was a fat man with a double chin like a woman's and a smooth, plump face, deceptively gentle-looking. The smell of fermentation clung to his clothes and skin. If he was in a good mood he would call for wine and move from genealogy into history—the Tribe history of my ancestors. Little had changed in hundreds of years. Warlords might rise and fall, clans flourish and disappear, but the trade of the Tribe in all the essentials of life went on forever. Except now Arai wanted to bring about change. All other powerful warlords worked with the Tribe. Only Arai wanted to destroy them.

Gosaburo's chins wobbled with laughter at the idea.

At first I was called on only as a spy, sent to overhear conversations in taverns and teahouses, ordered to climb over walls and roofs at night and listen to men confiding in their sons or their wives. I heard the townspeople's secrets and fears, the Yoshida clan's strategies for spring, the concerns at the castle about Arai's intentions beyond the borders and about peasant uprisings close to home. I went into the mountain villages, listened to those peasants, and identified the ringleaders.

One night Gosaburo clicked his tongue in disapproval at a long-overdue account. Not only had no payments been made, more goods had been ordered. The man's name was Furoda, a low-ranking warrior who had turned to farming to support his large family and his liking for the good things in life. Beneath his name I read the symbols that indicated the rising level of intimidation already used against him: A barn had been set alight, one of his daughters abducted, a son beaten up, dogs and horses killed. Yet, he still sank ever more deeply into the Kikuta's debt.

"This could be one for the Dog," the merchant said to Akio, who had joined us for a glass of wine. Like everyone except Yuki, he used Akio's nickname for me.

Akio took the scroll and ran his eyes over Furoda's sad history. "He's had a lot of leeway."

"Well, he's a likable fellow. I've known him since we were boys. I can't go on making allowances for him, though."

"Uncle, if you don't deal with him, isn't everyone going to expect the same leniency?" Akio said.

"That's the trouble: No one's paying on time at the moment. They all think they can get away with it because Furoda has." Gosaburo sighed deeply, his eyes almost disappearing in the folds of his cheeks. "I'm too softhearted. That's my problem. My brothers are always telling me."

"The Dog is softhearted," Akio said. "But we're training him not to be. He can take care of Furoda for you. It will be good for him."

"If you kill him he can never pay his debts," I said.

"But everyone else will." Akio spoke as if pointing out an obvious truth to a simpleton.

"It's often easier to claim from a dead man than a live one," Gosaburo added apologetically.

I did not know this easygoing, pleasure-loving, irresponsible man, and I did not want to kill him. But I did. A few days later I went at night to his house on the outskirts of town, silenced the dogs, went invisible, and slipped past the guards. The house was well barred but I waited for him outside the privy. I had been watching the house and I knew he always rose in the early hours to relieve himself. He was a large, fleshy man who'd long since given up any training and who had handed over the heavy work on the land to his sons. He'd grown soft. He died with hardly a sound.

When I untwisted the garrote, rain had started to fall. The tiles of the walls were slippery. The night was at its darkest. The rain could almost be sleet. I returned to the Kikuta house silenced by the darkness and the cold as if they had crept inside me and left a shadow on my soul.

Furoda's sons paid his debts, and Gosaburo was pleased with me. I let no one see how much the murder had disturbed me, but the next one was worse. It was on the orders of the Yoshida family. Determined to put a stop to the unrest among the villagers before winter, they put in a request for the leader to be eradicated. I knew the man, knew his secret fields, though I had not yet revealed them to anyone. Now I told Gosaburo and Akio where he could be found alone every evening, and they sent me to meet him there.

He had rice and sweet potatoes concealed in a small cave, cut into the side of the mountain and covered with stones and brushwood. He was working on the banks of the field when I came silently up the slope. I'd misjudged him: He was stronger than I thought, and he fought back with his hoe. As we struggled together, my hood slipped back and he saw my face. Recognition came into his eyes, mixed with a sort of horror. In that moment I used my second self, came behind him, and cut his throat, but I'd heard him call out to my image.

"Lord Shigeru!"

I was covered with blood, his and mine, and dizzy from the blow I'd not quite avoided. The hoe had glanced against my scalp and the scrape was bleeding freely. His words disturbed me deeply. Had he been calling to Shigeru's spirit for help, or had he seen my likeness and mistaken me for him? I wanted to question him, but his eyes stared blankly up at the twilight sky. He was beyond speech forever.

I went invisible and stayed so until I was nearly back at the Kikuta house, the longest period I had ever used it for. I would have stayed like that forever if I could. I could not forget the man's last words, and then I remembered what Shigeru had said, so long ago, in Hagi: *I have never killed an unarmed man, nor killed for pleasure.*

The clan lords were highly satisfied. The man's death had taken the heart out of the unrest. The villagers promptly became docile and obedient. Many of them would die of starvation before the end of winter. It was an excellent result, Gosaburo said.

But I began to dream of Shigeru every night. He entered the room and stood before me as if he had just come out of the river, blood and water streaming from him, saying nothing, his eyes fixed on me as if he were waiting for me— the same way he had waited with the patience of the heron for me to speak again.

Slowly it began to dawn on me that I could not bear the life I was living, but I did not know how to escape it. I had made a bargain with the Kikuta that I was now finding impossible to keep. I'd made the bargain in the heat of passion, not expecting to live beyond that night, and with no understanding of my own self. I'd thought the Kikuta master, who seemed to know me, would help me resolve the deep divisions and contradictions of my nature, but he had sent me away to Matsue with Akio, where my life with the Tribe might be teaching me how to hide these contradictions but was doing nothing to solve them; they were merely being driven deeper inside me.

My black mood worsened when Yuki went away. She said nothing to me about it, just vanished one day. In the morning I heard her voice and her tread while we were at training. I heard her go to the front door and leave without bidding anyone farewell. I listened all day for her return, but she did not come back. I tried asking casually where she was; the replies were evasive and I did not want to question Akio or Gosaburo directly. I missed her deeply but was also relieved that I no longer had to face the question of whether to sleep with her or not. Every day since she had told me about Kaede I'd resolved I would not, and every night I did.

Two days later, while I was thinking about her during the meditation period at the end of the morning exercises, I heard one of the servants come to the door and call softly to Akio. He opened his eyes slowly and, with the air of calm composure that he always assumed after meditating (and which I was convinced was only assumed), he rose and went to the door.

"The master is here," the girl said. "He is waiting for you."

"Hey, Dog," Akio called to me. The others sat without moving a muscle, without looking up, as I stood. Akio jerked his head and I followed him to the main room of the house, where Kikuta Kotaro was drinking tea with Gosaburo.

We entered the room and bowed to the floor before him.

"Sit up," he said, and studied me for a few moments. Then he addressed Akio. "Have there been any problems?"

"Not really," Akio said, implying there had been quite a few.

"What about attitude? You have no complaints?"

Akio shook his head slowly.

"Yet, before you left Yamagata . . . ?"

I felt that Kotaro was letting me know he knew everything about me.

"It was dealt with," Akio replied briefly.

"He's been quite useful to me," Gosaburo put in.

"I'm glad to hear it," Kotaro said dryly.

His brother got to his feet and excused himself—the pressures of business, the need to be in the shop. When he had left the master said, "I spoke to Yuki last night."

"Where is she?"

"That doesn't matter. But she told me something that disturbs me a little. We did not know that Shigeru went to Mino expressly to find you. He let Muto Kenji believe the encounter happened by chance."

He paused but I said nothing. I remembered the day Yuki had found this out, while she was cutting my hair. She had thought it important information, important enough to pass on to the master. No doubt she had told him everything else about me.

"It makes me suspect Shigeru had a greater knowledge of the Tribe than we realized," Kotaro said. "Is that true?"

"It's true that he knew who I was," I replied. "He had been friends with the Muto master for many years. That's all I know of his relationship with the Tribe."

"He never spoke to you of anything more?"

"No." I was lying. In fact Shigeru had told me more, the night we had talked in Tsuwano—that he had made it his business to find out about the Tribe and that he probably knew more about them than any other outsider. I had never shared this information with Kenji and I saw no reason to pass it on to Kotaro. Shigeru was dead, I was now bound to the Tribe, but I was not going to betray his secrets.

I tried to make my voice and face guileless and said, "Yuki asked me the same thing. What does it matter now?"

"We thought we knew Shigeru, knew his life," Kotaro answered. "He keeps surprising us, even after his death. He kept things hidden even from Kenji—the affair with Maruyama Naomi, for example. What else was he hiding?"

I shrugged slightly. I thought of Shigeru, nicknamed the Farmer, with his openhearted smile, his seeming frankness and simplicity. Everyone had misjudged him, especially the Tribe. He had been so much more than any of them had suspected.

"Is it possible that he kept records of what he knew about the Tribe?"

"He kept many records of all sorts of things," I said, sounding puzzled. "The seasons, his farming experiments, the land and crops, his retainers. Ichiro, his former teacher, helped him with them, but he often wrote himself."

I could see him, writing late into the night, the lamp

flickering, the cold penetrating, his face alert and intelligent, quite different from its usual bland expression.

"The journeys he made—did you go with him?"

"No, apart from our flight from Mino."

"How often did he travel?"

"I'm not sure; while I was in Hagi he did not leave the city."

Kotaro grunted. Silence crept into the room. I could barely hear the others' breathing. From beyond came the noon sounds of shop and house, the click of the abacus, the voices of customers, peddlers crying in the street outside. The wind was rising, whistling under the eaves, shaking the screens. Already its breath held the hint of snow.

The master spoke finally. "It seems most likely that he did keep records, in which case they must be recovered. If they should fall into Arai's hands at this moment, it would be a disaster. You will have to go to Hagi. Find out if the records exist and bring them back here."

I could hardly believe it. I had thought I would never go there again. Now I was to be sent back to the house I loved so much.

"It's a matter of the nightingale floor," Kotaro said. "I

believe Shigeru had one built around his house and you mastered it."

It seemed I was back there: I felt the heavy night air of the sixth month, saw myself run as silently as a ghost, heard Shigeru's voice: *Can you do it again?*

I tried to keep my face under control, but I felt a flicker in the smile muscles.

"You must leave at once," Kotaro went on. "You have to get there and back before the snows begin. It's nearly the end of the year. By the middle of the first month both Hagi and Matsue will be closed by snow."

He had not sounded angry before, but now I realized he was—profoundly. Perhaps he had sensed my smile.

"Why did you never tell anyone this?" he demanded. "Why did you keep it from Kenji?"

I felt my own anger rise in response. "Lord Shigeru did so and I followed his lead. My first allegiance was to him. I would never have revealed something he wanted kept secret. I was one of the Otori then, after all."

"And still thinks he is," Akio put in. "It's a question of loyalties. It always will be with him." He added under his breath, "A dog only knows one master."

I turned my gaze on him, willing him to look at me so I could shut him up, put him to sleep, but after one swift, contemptuous glance, he stared at the floor again.

"Well, that will be proved one way or the other," Kotaro replied. "I think this mission will test your loyalties to the full. If this Ichiro knows of the existence and contents of the records, he'll have to be removed, of course."

I bowed without saying anything, wondering if my heart had been hardened to the extent where I could kill Ichiro, the old man who had been Shigeru's teacher and then mine: I'd thought I wanted to often enough when he was chastising me and forcing me to learn, but he was one of the Otori, one of Shigeru's household. I was bound to him by duty and loyalty as well as by my own grudging respect and, I realized now, affection.

At the same time I was exploring the master's anger, feeling its taste in my mouth. It had a quality to it that was like Akio's more or less permanent state of rage against me, as if they both hated and feared me. "The Kikuta were delighted to discover Isamu had left a son," Kenji's wife had said. If they were so delighted why were they so angry with me? But hadn't she also said, "We all were"? And then Yuki had told me of her mother's old feelings for Shintaro. Could his death really have delighted her?

She had seemed at that moment like a garrulous old woman, and I had taken her words at face value. But moments later she'd allowed me a glimpse of her skills. She'd been flattering me, stroking my vanity in the same way she'd stroked my temples with her phantom hands. The reaction of the Kikuta to my sudden appearance was darker and more complex than they would have me believe: Maybe they were delighted with my skills, but there was also something about me that alarmed them, and I still did not understand what it was.

The anger that should have cowed me into obedience instead made me more stubborn—indeed, struck fire on that stubbornness and gave me energy. I felt it coiled inside me as I wondered at the fate that was sending me back to Hagi.

"We are entering a dangerous time," the master said, studying me as if he could read my thoughts. "The Muto house in Yamagata was searched and ransacked. Someone suspected you had been there. However, Arai has returned to Inuyama now, and Hagi is a long way from there. It's a risk for you to return, but the risk of records coming into anyone else's hands is far greater."

"What if they aren't in Lord Shigeru's house? They could be hidden anywhere."

"Presumably, Ichiro will know. Question him, and bring them back from wherever they are."

"Am I to leave immediately?"

"The sooner the better."

"As an actor?"

"No actors travel at this time of year," Akio said scornfully. "Besides, we will go alone."

I'd been offering a silent prayer that he would not be coming with me. The master said, "Akio will accompany you. His grandfather—your grandfather—has died, and you are returning to Hagi for the memorial service."

"I would prefer not to travel with Akio," I said.

Akio drew his breath in sharply. Kotaro said, "There are no preferences for you. Only obedience."

I felt the stubbornness spark, and looked directly at him. He was staring into my eyes as he had once before: He had put me to sleep immediately then. But this time I could meet his gaze without giving into it. There was something behind his eyes that made him flinch slightly from me. I searched his look and a suspicion leaped into my mind.

This is the man who killed my father.

I felt a moment of terror at what I was doing, then my own gaze steadied and held. I bared my teeth, though I was far from smiling. I saw the master's look of astonishment and saw his vision cloud. Then Akio was on his feet, striking me in the face, almost knocking me to the ground.

"How dare you do that to the master? You have no respect, you scum."

Kotaro said, "Sit down, Akio."

My eyes snapped back to him, but he was not looking at me.

"I'm sorry, master," I said softly. "Forgive me."

We both knew my apology was hollow. He stood swiftly and covered the moment with anger.

"Ever since we located you we have been trying to protect you from yourself." He did not raise his voice but there was no mistaking his fury. "Not only for your own sake, of course. You know what your talents are and how useful they could be to us. But your upbringing, your mixed blood, your own character, all work against you. I thought training here would help, but we don't have time to continue it. Akio will go with you to Hagi and you will continue to obey him in all things. He is far more experienced than you; he knows where the safe houses are, whom to contact and who can be trusted."

He paused while I bowed in acceptance, and then went on, "You and I made a bargain at Inuyama. You chose to disobey my orders then and return to the castle. The results of Iida's death have not been good for us. We were far better off under him than under Arai. Apart from our own laws of obedience that any child learns before they turn seven, your life is already forfeit to me by your own promise."

I did not reply. I felt he was close to giving up on me, that his patience with me, the understanding of my nature that had calmed and soothed me, was running dry. As was my trust in him. The terrible suspicion lay in my mind; once it had arisen there was no eradicating it: My father had died at the hands of the Tribe, maybe even killed by Kotaro himself, because he had tried to leave them. Later I would realize that this explained many things about the Kikuta's dealings with me—their insistence on my obedience, their ambivalent attitude to my skills, their contempt of my loyalty to Shigeru—but at that time it only increased my depression. Akio hated me, I had insulted and offended the Kikuta master, Yuki had left me, Kaede was probably dead . . . I did not want to go on

with the list. I gazed with unseeing eyes at the floor while
Kikuta and Akio discussed details of the journey.

We left the following morning. There were many travel-
ers on the road, taking advantage of the last weeks before the
snow fell, going home for the New Year Festival. We mingled
with them, two brothers returning to our hometown for a
funeral. It was no hardship to pretend to be overcome by
grief. It seemed to have become my natural state. The only
thing that lightened the blackness that enveloped me was the
thought of seeing the house in Hagi and hearing for one last
time its winter song.

My training partner, Hajime, traveled with us for the
first day; he was on his way to join a wrestling stable for the
winter to prepare for the spring tournaments. We stayed that
night with the wrestlers and ate the evening meal with them.
They consumed huge stews of vegetables and chicken, a meat
they considered lucky because the chicken's hands never
touch the ground, with noodles made of rice and buckwheat,
more for each one than most families would eat in a week.
Hajime, with his large bulk and calm face, resembled them

already. He had been connected with this stable, which was run by the Kikuta, since he was a child, and the wrestlers treated him with teasing affection.

Before the meal we bathed with them in the vast steamy bathhouse, built across a scalding, sulfurous spring. Masseurs and trainers mingled among them, rubbing and scrubbing the massive limbs and torsos. It was like being among a race of giants. They all knew Akio, of course, and treated him with ironic deference, because he was the boss's family, mixed with kindly scorn, because he was not a wrestler. Nothing was said about me, and nobody paid me any attention. They were absorbed in their own world. I obviously had only the slightest connection to it and therefore was of no interest to them.

So I said nothing, but listened. I overheard plans for the spring tournament, the hopes and desires of the wrestlers, the jokes whispered by the masseurs, the propositions made, spurned, or accepted. And much later, when Akio had ordered me to bed and I was already lying on a mat in the communal hall, I heard him and Hajime in the room below. They had decided to sit up for a while and drink together before they parted the next day.

I tuned out the snores of the wrestlers and concentrated

on the voices below. I could hear them clearly through the floor. It always amazed me that Akio seemed to forget how acute my hearing was. I supposed he did not want to acknowledge my gifts, and this made him underestimate me. At first I thought it was a weakness in him, almost the only one; later it occurred to me that there were some things he might have wanted me to hear.

The conversation was commonplace—the training Hajime would undergo, the friends they'd caught up with— until the wine began to loosen their tongues.

"You'll go to Yamagata, presumably?" Hajime asked.

"Probably not. The Muto master is still in the mountains, and the house is empty."

"I assumed Yuki had gone back to her family."

"No, she's gone to the Kikuta village, north of Matsue. She'll stay there until the child is born."

"The child?" Hajime sounded as dumbfounded as I was.

There was a long silence. I heard Akio drink and swallow. When he spoke again his voice was much quieter. "She is carrying the Dog's child."

Hajime hissed through his teeth. "Sorry, Cousin, I don't want to upset you, but was that part of the plan?"

"Why should it not have been?"

"I always thought, you and she . . . that you would marry eventually."

"We have been promised to each other since we were children," Akio said. "We may still marry. The masters wanted her to sleep with him, to keep him quiet, to distract him, to get a child if possible."

If he felt pain he was not showing it. "I was to pretend suspicion and jealousy," he said flatly. "If the Dog knew he was being manipulated, he might never have gone with her. Well, I did not have to pretend it: I did not realize she would enjoy it so much. I could not believe how she was with him, seeking him out day and night like a bitch in heat—" His voice broke off. I heard him gulp down a cup of wine and heard the clink and gurgle of the flask as more was poured.

"Good must come of it, though," Hajime suggested, his voice regaining some of its cheerfulness. "The child will inherit a rare combination of talents."

"So the Kikuta master thinks. And this child will be with us from birth. It will be raised properly, with none of the Dog's deficiencies."

"It's astonishing news," Hajime said. "No wonder you've been preoccupied."

"Most of the time I'm thinking about how I'll kill him," Akio confessed, drinking deeply again.

"You've been ordered to?" Hajime said bleakly.

"It all depends on what happens at Hagi. You might say he's on his last chance."

"Does he know that? That he's being tested?"

"If he doesn't, he'll soon find out," Akio said. After another long pause he said, "If the Kikuta had known of his existence, they would have claimed him as a child and brought him up. But he was ruined first by his upbringing and then by his association with the Otori."

"His father died before he was born. Do you know who killed him?"

"They drew lots," Akio whispered. "No one knows who actually did it, but it was decided by the whole family. The master told me this in Inuyama."

"Sad," Hajime murmured. "So much talent wasted."

"It comes from mixing the blood," Akio said. "It's true that it sometimes throws up rare talents, but they seem to come with stupidity. And the only cure for stupidity is death."

Shortly afterward they came to bed. I lay still, feigning sleep, until daybreak, my mind gnawing uselessly at the news. I was sure that no matter what I did or failed to do in Hagi, Akio would seize on any excuse to kill me there.

As we bade farewell to Hajime the next morning, he would not look me in the eye. His voice held a false cheerfulness, and he stared after us, his expression glum. I imagine he thought he would never see me again.

We traveled for three days, barely speaking to each other, until we came to the barrier that marked the beginning of the Otori lands. It presented no problem to us, Akio having been supplied with the necessary tablets of identification. He made all the decisions on our journey: where we should eat, where we should stop for the night, which road we should take. I followed passively. I knew he would not kill me before we got to Hagi; he needed me to get into Shigeru's house, across the nightingale floor. After a while I began to feel a sort of regret that we weren't good friends, traveling together. It seemed a waste of a journey. I longed for a companion, someone like Makoto or my old friend from Hagi, Fumio, with whom I could talk on the road and share the confusion of my thoughts.

Once we were in Otori land I expected the countryside to look as prosperous as it had when I had first traveled through it with Shigeru, but everywhere bore signs of the ravages of the storms and the famine that followed them. Many villages seemed to be deserted, damaged houses stood unrepaired, starving people begged at the side of the road. I overheard snatches of conversation: how the Otori lords were now demanding sixty percent of the rice harvest, instead of the forty percent they had taken previously, to pay for the army they were raising to fight Arai, and how men might as well kill themselves and their children rather than starve slowly to death when winter came.

Earlier in the year we might have made the journey more swiftly by boat, but the winter gales were already lashing the coast, driving foaming gray waves onto the black shore. The fishermen's boats were moored in such shelter as they could find, or pulled high onto the shingle, lived in by families until spring. Throughout winter the fishing families burned fires to get salt from the seawater. Once or twice we stopped to warm ourselves and eat with them, Akio paying them a few small coins. The food was meager: salt fish, soup made from kelp, sea urchins, and small shellfish.

One man begged us to buy his daughter, take her with us to Hagi, and use her ourselves or sell her to a brothel. She could not have been more than thirteen years old, barely into womanhood. She was not pretty, but I can still recall her face, her eyes both frightened and pleading, her tears, the look of relief when Akio politely declined, the despair in her father's attitude as he turned away.

That night Akio grumbled about the cold, regretting his decision. "She'd have kept me warm," he said more than once.

I thought of her sleeping next to her mother, faced with the choice between starvation and what would have been no more than slavery. I thought about Furoda's family, turned out of their shabby, comfortable house, and I thought of the man I'd killed in his secret field, and the village that would die because of me.

These things did not bother anyone else—it was the way the world was—but they haunted me. And of course, as I did every night, I took out the thoughts that had lain within me all day and examined them.

Yuki was carrying my child. It was to be raised by the Tribe. I would probably never even set eyes on it.

The Kikuta had killed my father because he had broken

the rules of the Tribe, and they would not hesitate to kill me.

I made no decisions and came to no conclusions. I simply lay awake for long hours of the night, holding the thoughts as I would hold black pebbles in my hand, and looking at them.

The mountains fell directly to the sea around Hagi, and we had to turn inland and climb steeply before we crossed the last pass and began the descent toward the town.

My heart was full of emotion, though I said nothing and gave nothing away. The town lay as it always had, in the cradle of the bay, encircled by its twin rivers and the sea. It was late afternoon on the day of the winter solstice, and a pale sun was struggling through gray clouds. The trees were bare, fallen leaves thick underfoot. Smoke from the burning of the last rice stalks spread a blue haze that hung above the rivers, level with the stone bridge.

Preparations were already being made for the New Year Festival: Sacred ropes of straw hung everywhere and dark-leaved pine trees had been placed by doorways; the shrines were filling with visitors. The river was swollen with the tide that was just past the turn and ebbing. It sang its wild song to me, and beneath its churning waters I seemed to hear the voice of the stonemason, walled up inside his creation, carrying on his endless conversation with the river. A heron rose from the shallows at our approach.

When we crossed the bridge I read again the inscription that Shigeru had read to me: *The Otori clan welcomes the just and the loyal. Let the unjust and the disloyal beware.*

Unjust and disloyal. I was both: disloyal to Shigeru, who had entrusted his lands to me, and unjust as the Tribe are, unjust and pitiless.

I walked through the streets, head down and eyes lowered, changing the set of my features in the way Kenji had taught me. I did not think anyone would recognize me. I had grown a little and had become both leaner and more muscular during the past months. My hair was cut short; my clothes were those of an artisan. My body language, my speech, my gait—everything about me was changed since the days when I'd walked through these streets as a young lord of the Otori clan.

We went to a brewery on the edge of town. I'd walked by it dozens of times in the past, knowing nothing of its real trade. *But,* I thought, *Shigeru would have known.* The idea pleased me: that he had kept track of the Tribe's activities, had known things that they were ignorant of, had known of my existence.

The place was busy with preparations for the winter's work. Huge amounts of wood were being gathered to heat the vats, and the air was thick with the smell of fermenting rice. We were met by a small, distracted man who resembled Kenji. He was from the Muto family; Yuzuru was his given name. He had not been expecting visitors so late in the year, and my presence and what we told him of our mission unnerved him. He took us hastily inside to another concealed room.

"These are terrible times," he said. "The Otori are certain to start preparing for war with Arai in the spring. It's only winter that protects us now."

"You've heard of Arai's campaign against the Tribe?"

"Everyone's talking about it," Yuzuru replied. "We've been told we should support the Otori against him as much as we can for that reason." He shot a look at me and said resentfully, "Things were much better under Iida. And surely it's a grave mistake to bring him here. If anyone should recognize him . . ."

"We'll be gone tomorrow," Akio replied. "He just has to retrieve something from his former home."

"From Lord Shigeru's? It's madness. He'll be caught."

"I don't think so. He's quite talented." I thought I heard mockery beneath the compliment and took it as one more indication that he meant to kill me.

Yuzuru stuck out his bottom lip. "Even monkeys fall from trees. What can be so important?"

"We think Otori might have kept extensive records on the Tribe's affairs."

"Shigeru? The Farmer? Impossible!"

Akio's eyes hardened. "Why do you think that?"

"Everyone knows . . . well, Shigeru was a good man. Everyone loved him. His death was a terrible tragedy. But he died because he was . . ." Yuzuru blinked furiously and looked apologetically at me. "He was too trusting. Innocent almost. He was never a conspirator. He knew nothing about the Tribe."

"We have reasons to think otherwise," Akio said. "We'll know who's right before tomorrow's dawn."

"You're going there tonight?"

"We must be back in Matsue before the snows come."

"Well, they'll be early this year, possibly before the year's end." Yuzuru sounded relieved to be talking about something as mundane as the weather. "All the signs are for a

long, hard winter. And if spring's going to bring war, I wish
it may never come."

It was already freezing within the small, dark room, the
third such that I had been concealed in. Yuzuru himself
brought us food, tea—already cooling by the time we tasted
it—and wine. Akio drank the wine but I did not, feeling I
needed my senses to remain acute. We sat without speaking
as night fell.

The brewery quieted around us, though its smell did not
diminish. I listened to the sounds of the town, each one so
familiar to me, I felt I could pinpoint the exact street, the
exact house, it came from. The familiarity relaxed me, and my
depression began to lift a little. The bell sounded from
Daishoin, the nearest temple, for the evening prayers. I could
picture the weathered building, the deep green darkness of
its grove, the stone lanterns that marked the graves of the
Otori lords and their retainers. I fell into a sort of waking
dream in which I was walking among them.

Then Shigeru came to me again as if from out of a white
mist, dripping with water and blood, his eyes burning black,
holding an unmistakable message for me. I snapped awake,
shivering with cold.

Akio said, "Drink some wine, it'll steady your nerves."

I shook my head, stood, and went through the limbering exercises the Tribe use until I was warm. Then I sat in meditation, trying to retain the heat, focusing my mind on the night's work, drawing together all my powers, knowing now how to do at will what I had once done by instinct.

From Daishoin the bell sounded. Midnight.

I heard Yuzuru approaching, and the door slid open. He beckoned to us and led us through the house to the outer gates. Here he alerted the guards and we went over the wall. One dog barked briefly but was silenced with a cuff.

It was pitch dark, the air icy, a raw wind blowing off the sea. On such a foul night no one was on the streets. We went silently to the riverbank and walked southeast toward the place where the rivers joined. The fish weir where I had often crossed to the other side lay exposed by the low tide. Just beyond it was Shigeru's house. On the near bank, boats were moored. We used to cross the river in them to his lands on the opposite side, the rice fields and farms, where he tried to teach me about agriculture and irrigation, crops, and coppices. And boats had brought the wood for the tearoom and the nightingale floor, listing low in the water with the sweet-smelling planks, freshly cut from the forests beyond the farms. Tonight it was too dark even to make out the mountain slopes where the trees had grown.

We crouched by the side of the narrow road and looked at the house. There were no lights visible, just the dim glow of a brazier from the guardroom at the gate. I could hear men and dogs breathing deeply in sleep. The thought crossed my mind: They would not have slept so had Shigeru been alive. I was angry on his behalf, not least with myself.

Akio whispered, "You know what you have to do?"

I nodded.

"Go, then."

We made no other plans. He simply sent me off as if I were a falcon or a hunting dog. I had a fair idea what his own plan was: When I returned with the records, he would take them—and I would be reported unfortunately killed by the guards, my body thrown into the river.

I crossed the street, went invisible, leaped over the wall, and dropped into the garden. Immediately the muffled song of the house enveloped me: the sighing of the wind in the trees, the murmur of the stream, the splash of the waterfall, the surge of the river as the tide began to flow. Sorrow swept over me. What was I doing returning here in the night like a thief? Almost unconsciously I let my face change, let my Otori look return.

The nightingale floor extended around the whole house, but it held no threat to me. Even in the dark I could still cross it without making it sing. On the farther side I climbed the wall to the window of the upper room—the same route the Tribe assassin, Shintaro, had taken over a year ago. At the top I listened. The room seemed empty.

The shutters were closed against the freezing night air, but they were not bolted, and it was easy to slide them apart enough to creep through. Inside it was barely any warmer and even darker. The room smelled musty and sour, as if it had been closed for a long time, as if no one sat there anymore save ghosts.

I could hear the household breathing and recognized the sleep of each one. But I could not place the one I needed to find: Ichiro. I stepped down the narrow staircase, knowing its favorite creaks as I knew my own hands. Once below I realized the house was not completely dark as it had appeared from the street. In the farthest room, the one Ichiro favored, a lamp was burning. I went quietly toward it. The paper screen was closed, but the lamp threw the shadow of the old man onto it. I slid open the door.

He raised his head and looked at me without surprise. He smiled sorrowfully and made a slight movement with his hand. "What can I do for you? You know I would do anything to bring you peace, but I am old. I have used the pen more than the sword."

"Teacher," I whispered. "It's me. Takeo." I stepped into the room, slid the door closed behind me, and dropped to my knees before him.

He gave a shudder as if he had been asleep and just woken, or as if he had been in the world of the dead and been called back by the living. He grabbed my shoulders and pulled me toward him, into the lamplight. "Takeo? Can it really be you?" He ran his hands over my head, my limbs, as though fearing I were an apparition, tears trickling down his cheeks. Then he embraced me, cradling my head against his shoulder as if I were his long-lost son. I could feel his thin chest heaving.

He pulled back a little and gazed into my face. "I thought you were Shigeru. He often visits me at night. He stands there in the doorway. I know what he wants, but what can I do?" He wiped the tears away with his sleeve. "You've grown like him. It's quite uncanny. Where have you been all this time? We thought you, too, must have been murdered, except that every few weeks someone comes to the house looking for you, so we assumed you were still alive."

"I was hidden by the Tribe," I said, wondering how much he knew of my background. "First in Yamagata, for the last two months in Matsue. I made a bargain with them. They kidnapped me at Inuyama but released me to go into the castle and bring Lord Shigeru out. In return I agreed to enter their service. You may not know that I am bound to them by blood."

"Well, I'd assumed it," Ichiro said. "Why else would Muto Kenji have turned up here?" He took my hand and pressed it with emotion. "Everyone knows the story of how you rescued Shigeru and slew Iida in revenge. I don't mind telling you, I always thought he was making a grave mistake adopting you, but you silenced all my misgivings and paid all your debts to him that night."

"Not quite all. The Otori lords betrayed him to Iida and they are still unpunished."

"Is that what you have come for? That would bring rest to his spirit."

"No, I was sent by the Tribe. They believe Lord Shigeru kept records on them and they want to retrieve them."

Ichiro smiled wryly. "He kept records of many things. I go through them every night. The Otori lords claim your adoption was not legal and that anyway you are probably dead, therefore Shigeru has no heirs and his lands must revert to the castle. I've been looking for more proof so that you may keep what is yours." His voice became stronger and more urgent. "You must come back, Takeo. Half the clan will support you for what you did in Inuyama. Many suspect that Shigeru's uncles planned his death and are outraged by it. Come back and finish your revenge!"

Shigeru's presence was all around us. I expected him at any moment to walk into the room with his energetic step, his openhearted smile, and the dark eyes that looked so frank yet hid so much.

"I feel I must," I said slowly. "I will have no peace unless I do. But the Tribe will certainly try to kill me if I desert them—more than try; they will not rest until they have succeeded."

Ichiro took a deep breath. "I don't believe I have mis-judged you," he said. "If I have, you came prepared to kill me anyway. I am old, I am ready to move on. But I would like to see Shigeru's work finished. It's true, he did keep records on the Tribe. He believed no one could bring peace to the Middle Country while the Tribe were so strong, so he devoted himself to finding out all he could about them and he wrote it all down. He made sure no one knew what was in his records, not even me. He was extremely secretive, far more than anyone ever realized. He had to be; for ten years both Iida and his uncles had tried to get rid of him."

"Can you give them to me?"

"I will not give them back to the Tribe," he said. The lamp flickered, suddenly sending a crafty look across his face that I had never seen before. "I must get more oil or we'll be sitting in darkness. Let me wake Chiyo."

"Better not," I said, even though I would have loved to have seen the old woman who ran the house and treated me like a son. "I can't stay."

"Did you come alone?"

I shook my head. "Kikuta Akio is waiting for me outside."

"Is he dangerous?"

"He's almost certainly going to try to kill me. Especially if I return to him empty-handed." I was wondering what hour it was, what Akio was doing. The house's winter song was all around me. I did not want to leave it. My choices seemed to be narrowing. Ichiro would never hand the records over to the Tribe; I would never be able to kill him to get them. I took my knife from my sash, felt its familiar weight in my hand. "I should take my own life now."

"Well, it would be one answer," Ichiro said, and sniffed. "But not a very satisfactory one. I would then have two unquiet ghosts visiting me in the night. And Shigeru's murderers would go unpunished."

The lamp spluttered. Ichiro stood. "I'll get more oil," he muttered. I listened to him shuffling through the house and thought about Shigeru. How many nights would he have sat until late in this very room? Boxes of scrolls stood around me. As I gazed idly at them I suddenly remembered with complete clarity the wooden chest that I had carried up the slope as a gift for the abbot on the day we had visited the temple to see the Sesshu paintings. I thought I saw Shigeru smile at me.

When Ichiro had returned and fixed the lamp, he said, "Anyway, the records aren't here."

"I know," I said. "They are at Terayama."

Ichiro grinned. "If you want my advice, even though you never took any notice of it in the past, go there. Go now, tonight. I'll give you money for the journey. They'll hide you for the winter. And from there you can plan your revenge on the Otori lords. That's what Shigeru wants."

"It's what I want, too. But I made a bargain with the Kikuta master. I am bound to the Tribe now by my word."

"I think you swore allegiance to the Otori first," Ichiro said. "Didn't Shigeru save your life before the Tribe had even heard of you?"

I nodded.

"And you said Akio would kill you? They have already broken faith with you. Can you get past him? Where is he?"

"I left him in the road outside. He could be anywhere now."

"Well, you can hear him first, can't you? And what about those tricks you used to play on me? Always somewhere else when I thought you were studying."

"Teacher . . ." I began. I was going to apologize but he waved me silent.

"I forgive you everything. It was not my teaching that enabled you to bring Shigeru out of Inuyama."

He left the room again and came back with a small string of coins and some rice cakes wrapped in kelp. I had no carrying cloth or box to put them in, and anyway I was going to need both hands free. I tied the money into my loincloth beneath my clothes and put the rice cakes in my belt.

"Can you find the way?" he said, starting to fuss as he used to in the past over a shrine visit or some other outing.

"I think so."

"I'll write you a letter to get you through the barrier. You're a servant of this household—it's what you look like—making arrangements for my visit to the temple next year. I'll meet you in Terayama when the snows melt. Wait for me there. Shigeru was in alliance with Arai. I don't know how things stand between you, but you should seek Arai's protection. He will be grateful for any information he can use against the Tribe."

He took up the brush and wrote swiftly. "Can you still write?" he asked, without looking up.

"Not very skillfully."

"You'll have all winter to practice." He sealed the letter and stood. "By the way, what happened to Jato?"

"It came into my hands. It's being kept for me at Terayama."

"Time to go back for it." He smiled again and grumbled, "Chiyo's going to kill me for not waking her."

I slipped the letter inside my clothes and we embraced.

"Some strange fate ties you to this house," he said. "I believe it is a bond you cannot escape." His voice broke and I saw he was close to tears again.

"I know it," I whispered. "I will do everything you suggest." I knew I could not give up this house and inheritance. They were mine. I would reclaim them. Everything Ichiro had said made perfect sense. I had to escape from the Tribe. Shigeru's records would protect me from them and give me bargaining power with Arai. If I could only get to Terayama . . .

· 2 ·

I left the house the same way I had come, out through the upstairs window, down the wall, and across the nightingale floor. It slept under my feet, but I vowed next time I walked on it I would make it sing. I did not scale the wall back into the street. Instead, I ran silently through the garden, went invisible, and, clinging like a spider to the stones, climbed through the opening where the stream flowed into the river. I dropped into the nearest boat, untied it, took up the oar that lay in the stern, and pushed off into the river.

The boat groaned slightly under my weight, and the current lapped more strongly at it. To my dismay the sky had cleared. It was much colder and, under the three-quarters moon, much brighter. I heard the thud of feet from the bank, sent my image back to the wall, and crouched low in the boat. But Akio was not deceived by my second self. He leaped from the wall as if he were flying. I went invisible again, even though I knew it was probably useless against him, bounded from my boat, and flew low across the surface of the water into another of the boats that lay against the river wall. I scrabbled to undo its rope and pushed off with its oar. I saw Akio land and steady himself against the rocking of the craft; then he sprang and flew again as I split myself, left the second self in one boat, and leaped for the other. I felt the air shift as we passed each other. Controlling my fall, I dropped into my first boat, took up the oar, and began to scull faster than I ever had in my life. My second self faded as Akio grasped it, and I saw him prepare to leap again. There was no escape unless I went into the river. I drew my knife and as he landed stabbed at him with one hand. He moved with his usual speed and ducked easily under the knife. I had anticipated his move and caught him on the side of the head with the oar. He fell, stunned for a moment, while I, thrown off balance by the violent rocking of the boat, narrowly escaped tumbling overboard. I dropped the oar and clung to the wooden side. I did not want to go into the freezing water unless I took him with me and drowned him. As I slid to the other side of the boat Akio recovered. He leaped straight upward and came down on top of me. We fell together and he seized me by the throat.

I was still invisible but helpless, pinned under him like a carp on the cook's slab. I felt my vision blacken; then he loosened his grip slightly.

"You traitor," he said. "Kenji warned us you would go back to the Otori in the end. I'm glad you did, because I've wanted you dead since the first time we met. You're going to pay now. For your insolence to the Kikuta, for my hand. And for Yuki."

"Kill me," I said, "as your family killed my father. You will never escape our ghosts. You will be cursed and haunted till the day you die. You murdered your own kin."

The boat moved beneath us, drifting with the tide. If Akio had used his hands or knife then, I would not be telling this story. But he couldn't resist one last taunt. "Your child will be mine. I'll bring him up properly as a real Kikuta." He shook me violently. "Show me your face," he snarled. "I want to see your look when I tell you how I'll

LIAN HEARN

teach him to hate your memory. I want to watch you die."

He leaned closer, his eyes searching for my face. The boat drifted into the path of the moon. As I saw its brightness I let visibility return and looked straight into his eyes. I saw what I wanted to find: the jealous hatred of me that clouded his judgment and weakened him.

He realized in a split second and tried to wrench his gaze away but the blow from the oar must have slowed his usual quickness and it was too late. He was already made dizzy by the encroaching Kikuta sleep. He slumped sideways, his eyelids flickering erratically as he fought it. The boat tipped and rocked. His own weight took him headfirst into the river.

The boat drifted on, faster now, carried by the swelling tide. In the moonlit road across the water I saw the body surface. It floated gently. I was not going to go back and finish him off. I hoped he'd drown or freeze to death but I left it to fate. I took up the oar and sculled the boat to the far shore.

By the time I got there I was shivering with cold. The first roosters were crowing and the moon was low in the sky. The grass on the bank was stiff with frost and stones and twigs gleamed white. I disturbed a sleeping heron and wondered if

60

it was the one that came to fish in Shigeru's garden. It flew off from the highest branches of the willow with the familiar clack of wings.

I was exhausted but far too wrought up to think of sleep, and anyway I had to keep moving to warm myself. I forced myself to a quick pace, following the narrow mountain road toward the southeast. The moon was bright and I knew the track. By daybreak I was over the first pass and on my way down to a small village. Hardly anyone was stirring, but an old woman was blowing up the embers in her hearth and she heated some soup for me in return for one of the coins. I complained to her about my senile old master sending me off on a wild-goose chase through the mountains to a remote temple. The winter would undoubtedly finish him off and I'd be stranded there.

She cackled and said, "You'll have to become a monk, then!"

"Not me. I like women too much."

This pleased her, and she found some freshly pickled plums to add to my breakfast. When she saw my string of coins she wanted to give me lodging as well as food. Eating had brought the sleep demon closer, and I longed to lie down, but I was too afraid of being recognized and I already regretted I had said as much as I had to her. I might have left Akio in the river, but I knew how the river gives up its victims, both the living and the dead, and I feared his pursuit. I was not proud of my defection from the Tribe after I had sworn to obey them, and in the cold light of morning I was beginning to realize what the rest of my life would be like. I had made my choice to return to the Otori, but now I would never be free from the dread of assassination. An entire secret organization would be drawn up against me to punish me for my disloyalty. To slip through their web, I had to move faster than any of their messengers would. And I had to get to Terayama before it began to snow.

The sky had turned the color of lead when I reached Tsuwano on the afternoon of the second day. My thoughts were all of my meeting there with Kaede and the sword-training session when I had fallen in love with her. Was her name already entered in the ledgers of the dead? Would I have to light candles for her now every year at the Festival of the Dead until I died? Would we be joined in the afterworld, or were we condemned never to meet again either in life or in death? Grief and shame gnawed at me. She had said, "I only feel safe with you," and I had abandoned her. If fate were to be kind and she were to come into my hands again, I would never let her go.

I regretted bitterly my decision to go with the Tribe, and I went over the reasons behind my choice many times. I believed I had made a bargain with them and my life was forfeit to them—that was one thing. But beyond that I blamed my own vanity. I had wanted to know and develop the side of my character that came from my father, from the Kikuta, from the Tribe: the dark inheritance that gave me skills I was proud of. I had responded eagerly and willingly to their seduction, the mixture of flattery, understanding, and brutality with which they had used and manipulated me. I wondered how much chance I had to get away from them.

My thoughts went round and round in circles. I was walking in a kind of daze. I'd slept a little in the middle of the day in a hollow off the side of the road, but the cold woke me. The only way to stay warm was to keep walking. I skirted the town and, descending through the pass, picked up the road again near the river. The current had subsided from the full flood caused by the storms that had delayed us in Tsuwano, and the banks had been mended, but the bridge here, a wooden one, was still in ruins. I paid a boatman to take me across. No one else was traveling so late; I was his last customer. I felt he was eyeing me curiously but he did not speak to me. I could not place him as Tribe but he made me uneasy. He dropped me on the other side and I walked quickly away. When I turned at the corner of the road, he was still watching me. I made a movement with my head but he did not acknowledge it.

It was colder than ever, the air dank and icy. I was already regretting that I had not found shelter for the night. If I was caught by a blizzard before the next town, I stood little chance of surviving. Yamagata was still several days away. There would be a post station at the fief border, but, despite Ichiro's letter and my disguise as a servant, I did not want to spend the night there—too many curious people, too many guards. I didn't know what to do, so I kept walking.

Night fell. Even with my Tribe-trained eyes it was hard to see the road. Twice I wandered off it and had to retrace my steps. Once I stumbled into some sort of hole or ditch with water at the bottom, soaking my legs up to the knees. The wind howled and strange sounds came from the woods, reminding me of legends of monsters and goblins and making me think the dead walked behind me.

By the time the sky began to pale in the east, I was frozen to the bone and shivering uncontrollably. I was glad to see the dawn but it gave no relief from the bitter cold. Instead it just brought home to me how alone I was. For the first time the idea crept insidiously into my head that if the fief border was manned by Arai's men, I would give myself up to them. They would take me to Arai, but first they would surely give me something hot to drink. They would sit me down inside by the fire and make tea for me. I became obsessed by the thought of that tea. I could feel the heat of the steam on my face, the warmth of the bowl in my hands. I was so obsessed by it that I did not notice someone walking behind me.

I was aware suddenly of a presence at my back. I turned, astonished that I had not heard the footfall on the road, had not even heard breathing. I was amazed, even frightened, at my apparent loss of hearing. It was as though this traveler had fallen from the sky or walked above the ground as the dead do. Then I knew that either exhaustion had unhinged my mind or I was indeed seeing a ghost, for the man walking just behind me was the outcast Jo-An, who I thought had been tortured to death by Arai's men in Yamagata.

So great was the shock, I thought I would faint. The blood rushed from my head, making me stagger. Jo-An grabbed me as I fell, his hands seeming real enough, strong and solid, smelling of the tannery. Earth and sky turned around me and black spots darkened my sight. He lowered me to the ground and pushed my head between my knees. Something was roaring in my ears, deafening me. I crouched like that, his hands holding my head, until the roaring lessened and the dark receded from my vision. I stared at the ground. The grass was rimed by frost, and tiny particles of black ice lay between each stone. The wind howled in the cedars. Apart from that, the only sound was my teeth chattering.

Jo-An spoke. There was no doubt; it was his voice. "Forgive me, lord. I startled you. I didn't mean to alarm you."

"They told me you were dead. I didn't know if you were a living being or a ghost."

"Well, I might have died for a while," he whispered. "Arai's men thought so and threw my body out in the marsh-land. But the Secret God had other plans for me and sent me back to this world. My work here is not yet done."

I lifted my head carefully and looked at him. He had a

new scar, not long healed, from nose to ear, and several teeth missing. I took his wrist and brought his hand round so I could see it. The nails were gone, the fingers clubbed and twisted.

"I should be asking your forgiveness," I said, sickened.

"Nothing happens to us that is not planned by God," he replied.

I wondered why any god's plans had to include torture, but I did not say this to Jo-An. Instead I asked, "How did you find me?"

"The boatman came to me and told me he had ferried someone he thought was you across the river. I've been waiting for word of you. I knew you would come back." He took up the bundle he'd placed by the side of the road and began to untie it. "The prophecy has to be fulfilled, after all."

"What prophecy?" I remembered that Kenji's wife had called him the lunatic.

He didn't answer. He took two small millet cakes from the cloth, prayed over them, and gave one to me.

"You are always feeding me," I said. "I don't think I can eat."

"Drink, then," Jo-An said, and handed me a rough bamboo flask. I wasn't sure about drinking, either, but I thought it might warm me. As soon as the liquor hit my stomach the darkness came roaring back, and I vomited several times so hard I was racked by violent shuddering.

Jo-An clicked his tongue as you would to a horse or an ox. He had the patient touch of a man used to dealing with animals, though of course he dealt with them at the moment of their death and then, afterward, flayed their corpses. When I could speak again I said through chattering teeth, "I must keep moving."

"Where are you heading?" he asked.

"Terayama. I'll spend the winter there."

"Well," he said, and fell into one of his familiar silences. He was praying, listening to some inner voice that would tell him what to do. "It's good," he said finally. "We'll go over the mountain. If you go by road they'll stop you at the barrier, and anyway it will take too long; it will snow before you get to Yamagata."

"Over the mountain?" I looked up at the jagged peaks that stretched away to the northeast. The road from Tsuwano to Yamagata skirted around their foot, but Terayama itself lay directly behind them. Around the range the clouds hung low and gray, with the dull damp sheen that presages snow.

"It's a steep climb," Jo-An said. "You must rest a little before you attempt it."

I began to think about getting to my feet. "I don't have time. I must get to the temple before it snows."

Jo-An looked up at the sky and sniffed the wind. "It will be too cold to snow tonight, but it could well start tomorrow. We'll ask the Secret One to hold it back."

He stood and helped me up. "Can you walk now? It's not far back to the place I live. You can rest there, then I'll take you to the men who will show you the way over the mountains."

I felt faint, as though my body had lost its substance, almost as though I'd split myself and somehow gone with my image. I was thankful for the Tribe training that had taught me to find those reserves of strength of which most men are unaware. Slowly as I concentrated my breathing I felt some energy and toughness return. Jo-An no doubt attributed my recovery to the power of his prayers. He regarded me for a moment with his deep-sunk eyes, then turned with a flicker of a smile and began to walk back the way we had come.

I hesitated for a moment, partly because I hated the thought of retracing my steps, losing the ground it had cost me so much to cover, but also because I recoiled from going with the outcast. It was one thing to talk with him at night, alone, quite another to walk close to him, to be seen in his company. I reminded myself that I was not yet an Otori lord, and no longer one of the Tribe, that Jo-An was offering me help and shelter, but my skin crawled as I followed him.

After walking for less than an hour we turned off the road onto a smaller path that followed the banks of a narrow river, through a couple of miserable villages. Children ran out to beg for food, but they backed away when they recognized the outcast. In the second village two older boys were bold enough to throw stones. One of them nearly struck me on the back—I heard the blow coming in time to step aside— and I was going to go back and punish the brat, but Jo-An restrained me.

Long before we reached it I could smell the tannery. The river widened and eventually flowed into the main channel. At the confluence stood the rows of wooden frames, skins stretched on them. Here in this damp sheltered spot they were protected from frost, but as winter's bite strengthened they would be taken down and stored till spring. Men were already at work, all outcasts of course, half-naked despite the cold, all as skeletally thin as Jo-An and with the same beaten look like mistreated dogs. Mist hung on the river, mingled with smoke from charcoal fires. A floating bridge, made of reeds and bamboo lashed together with cords, had been constructed across the river. I remembered Jo-An telling me to come to the outcasts' bridge if I ever needed help. Now some fate had brought me here; he would say the power of the Secret God, no doubt.

On the far side of the frames a few small wooden huts had been erected. They looked as if one strong wind would flatten them. As I followed Jo-An to the threshold of the nearest one, the men continued their work, but I was aware of their gaze. Each one looked at me with a kind of intense entreaty, as though I meant something to them and could help them in some way.

Trying to mask my reluctance, I stepped inside, not needing to remove my shoes as the floor was earthen. A small fire burned in the hearth. The air was thick with smoke, making my eyes sting. There was one other person inside, huddled in the corner, under a pile of hides. I thought it was Jo-An's wife until he came forward on his knees and bowed his head to the dirt before me. It was the man who had ferried me across the river.

."He walked most of the night to tell me he'd seen you," Jo-An said apologetically. "He needed to rest a little before returning."

I was aware of the sacrifice it entailed, not only the lonely walk through the goblin-haunted darkness, but the danger from robbers and patrols and the loss of a day's fees.

"Why did he do this for me?"

The boatman sat up then, raising his eyes and looking briefly at me. He said nothing, but the look he gave me was the same one I'd seen in the gaze of the tannery workers, a look of passion and hunger. I had seen it before, months earlier, on the faces of people as we rode back from Terayama to Yamagata, the look they threw out like an appeal to Shigeru. They had found in Shigeru the promise of something—justice, compassion—and now these men looked for the same thing in me. Whatever Jo-An had told them about me had transformed me into their hope.

And something in me responded to this, just as it had to the villagers, to the farmers with their hidden fields. They were treated like dogs, beaten and starved, but I saw them as men, with the brains and hearts of men, no less than any warrior or merchant. I had been brought up among people like them and been taught that the Secret God saw them all with equal eyes. No matter what I became, no matter what other teaching I received from the Otori or the Tribe—despite my own reluctance, even—it was impossible for me to forget this.

Jo-An said, "He is your man now. As I am—as we all are. You only have to call on us." He grinned, his broken teeth flashing in the dim light. He had made tea and handed me a small wooden bowl. I felt the steam rise against my face. The tea was made from twigs, such as we used to drink in Mino.

"Why should I call on you? What I'm going to need is an army!" I drank and felt the warmth begin to spread through me.

"Yes, an army," Jo-An replied. "Many battles lie ahead of you. The prophecy says it."

"How can you help me, then? It is forbidden for you to kill."

"Warriors will kill," Jo-An replied, "but there are many things they won't do that are equally necessary—things they consider beneath them: building, slaughtering, burying. You'll realize it when you need us."

The tea settled my stomach. Jo-An brought out two

more small millet balls, but I had no appetite and made the boatman eat my share. Jo-An did not eat, either, but put the second ball away again. I saw the other man's eyes follow it and gave him some coins before he left. He did not want to take them, but I pressed them into his hand.

Jo-An mumbled the blessing of departure over him and then pulled aside the hides so I could take his place under them. The warmth of the tea stayed with me. The hides stank, but they kept out the cold and muffled sound. I thought briefly how any one of those starving men might betray me for a bowl of soup, but I had no alternative now: I had to trust Jo-An. I let the darkness fall over me and take me down into sleep.

He woke me a few hours later. It was well after noon. He gave me tea, hardly more than hot water, and apologized for having no food to offer me.

"We should leave now," he said, "if we are to get to the charcoal burners before dark."

"The charcoal burners?" I usually woke swiftly, but this day I was groggy with sleep.

"They are still on the mountain. They have paths they use through the forest that will take you over the border. But they will leave with the first snow." He paused for a moment and then said, "We have to speak to someone on the way."

"Who?"

"It won't take long." He gave me one of his slight smiles. We went outside and I knelt by the riverbank and splashed water on my face. It was icy; as Jo-An had predicted, the temperature had dropped and the air was drier. It was too cold and too dry to snow.

I shook the water from my hands while he spoke to the men. Their eyes flickered toward me. When we left, they stopped work and knelt with bowed heads as I walked past.

"They know who I am?" I asked Jo-An in a low voice. Again, I feared betrayal from these men who had so little.

"They know you are Otori Takeo," he replied, "the angel of Yamagata who will bring justice and peace. That's what the prophecy says."

"What prophecy?" I asked again.

He said, "You will hear it for yourself."

I was filled with misgivings. What was I doing, entrusting my life to this lunatic? I felt every extra moment wasted would keep me from reaching Terayama before either the snow or the Tribe caught up with me. But I realized now that my only hope was to go over the mountain. I had to follow Jo-An.

We crossed the smaller river a little way upstream by a fish weir. We passed few people, a couple of fishermen, and some girls taking food to the men who were burning rice stalks and spreading dung on the empty fields. The girls climbed up the bank rather than cross our path, and one of the fisherman spat at us. The other cursed Jo-An for blighting the water. I kept my head low and my face averted, but they paid no attention to me. In fact they avoided looking at us directly, as though even that contact would bring pollution and bad luck.

Jo-An seemed to take no notice of the hostility, retreating into himself as if into a dark cloak, but when we had passed them he said, "They would not allow us to use the wooden bridge to take the hides across. That's why we had to learn to build our own. Now the other bridge is destroyed, but they still refuse to use ours." He shook his head and whispered, "If only they knew the Secret One."

On the other bank we followed the river for another mile and then turned off toward the northeast and began to climb. The bare-branched maples and beeches gave way to pines and cedars. As the forest deepened, the path darkened and grew steeper and steeper until we were clambering over rocks and boulders, going as often on all fours as upright. The sleep had refreshed me and I could feel strength returning. Jo-An climbed tirelessly, hardly even panting. It was hard to guess his age. Poverty and suffering had hollowed him out so he looked like an old man, but he might have been no more than thirty. There was something unearthly about him, as though he had indeed returned from the dead.

We finally came over a crest and stood on a small plateau. A huge rock lay across it, fallen from the crag above. Below us I could see the glint of the river, almost as far as Tsuwano. Smoke and mist drifted across the valley. The clouds were low, hiding the mountain range on the opposite side. The climb had warmed us, even made us sweat, but when we stopped our breath came white on the raw air. A few late berries still glowed red on leafless bushes; otherwise there was no color anywhere. Even the evergreen trees were muted almost to black. I could hear water trickling, and two crows were calling to each other from the crag. When they fell silent I heard someone breathing.

The sound came, slow and measured, from the rock

itself. I slowed my own breathing, touched Jo-An on the arm, and made a gesture with my head toward it.

He gave me a smile and spoke quietly: "It's all right. This is who we have come to see."

The crows cawed again, their voices harsh and ominous. I began to shiver. The cold was creeping up on me, surrounding me. The fears of the previous night threatened to surface again. I wanted to keep moving. I did not want to meet whoever was concealed behind the rock, breathing so slowly they could hardly be human.

"Come," Jo-An said, and I followed him round the edge of the rock, keeping my eyes away from the drop below. Behind, a cave was hollowed out of the side of the mountain. Water dripped from its roof. Over the centuries it had formed spears and columns and worn out a channel on the ground that led to a small deep pool, its sides as regular as a cistern and limestone-white. The water itself was black.

The roof of the cave sloped, following the shape of the mountain, and in the upper, drier side sat a figure that I would have thought was a statue if I had not heard its breathing. It was grayish white, like the limestone, as though it had sat there so long it had started to calcify. It was hard to tell if it was male or female; I recognized it as one of those ancient people, a hermit, a monk or nun, who had gone beyond sex and gender and grown so close to the next world he or she was almost pure spirit. The hair fell like a white shawl, the face and hands gray like old paper.

The figure sat in meditation on the floor of the cave with no sign of strain or discomfort. In front of it was a kind of stone altar bearing fading flowers, the last of the autumn lilies, and other offerings: two bitter oranges, their skins wrinkling, a small piece of fabric, and some coins of little value. It was like any other shrine to the god of the mountain, except carved into the stone was the sign the Hidden use, the one Lady Maruyama had traced on my hand in Chigawa so long ago.

Jo-An untied his cloth and took out the last millet cake. He knelt and placed it carefully on the altar, then bowed his head to the ground. The figure opened its eyes and gazed on us—gazed but did not see. The eyes were clouded with blindness. An expression came over the face that made me drop to my knees and bow before it—a look of profound tenderness and compassion, blended with complete knowledge. I had no doubt I was in the presence of a holy being.

"Tomasu," it said, and I thought its voice a woman's rather than a man's. It was so long since anyone had called me by the water name my mother gave me that the hair on the back of my neck stood up, and when I shivered it was not only from cold.

"Sit up," she said. "I have words to say that you are to hear. You are Tomasu of Mino, but you have become both Otori and Kikuta. Three bloods are mixed in you. You were born into the Hidden, but your life has been brought into the open and is no longer your own. Earth will deliver what heaven desires."

She fell silent. The minutes passed. The cold entered my bones. I wondered if she would say anything else. At first I was amazed that she knew who I was; then I thought Jo-An must have told her about me. If this was the prophecy, it was so obscure that it meant nothing to me. If I knelt there much longer I thought I would freeze to death, but I was held by the force of the blind woman's eyes.

I listened to the breath of the three of us and to the sounds of the mountain, the crows still cawing in their harsh voices, the cedars restless in the northeast wind, the trickle and drip of water, the groaning of the mountain itself as the temperature dropped and the rocks shrank.

"Your lands will stretch from sea to sea," she said finally. "But peace comes at the price of bloodshed. Five battles will buy you peace, four to win and one to lose. Many must die, but you yourself are safe from death, except at the hands of your own son."

Another long silence followed. With every second the light darkened toward evening and the air chilled. My gaze wandered round the cave. At the holy woman's side stood a prayer wheel on a small wooden block carved with lotus leaves around its edge. I was puzzled. I knew many mountain shrines were forbidden to women, and none I had ever seen had contained such a mixture of symbols, as though the Secret God, the Enlightened One, and the spirits of the mountain all dwelt here together.

She spoke as if she saw my thoughts; her voice held a kind of laughter mixed with wonder. "It is all one. Keep this in your heart. It is all one."

She touched the prayer wheel and set it turning. Its rhythm seemed to steal into my veins to join my blood. She began to chant softly, words I had never heard before and did not understand. They flowed over and around us, eventually fading into the wind. When we heard them again they had become the farewell blessing of the Hidden. She handed us a bowl and told us to drink from the pool before we left.

A thin layer of ice was already forming on the surface, and the water was so cold it bit into my teeth. Jo-An wasted no time but led me quickly away, glancing anxiously toward the north. Before we went back over the crest I took one last look at the holy woman. She sat motionless; from this distance she seemed like part of the rock. I could not believe she would stay out here alone all night.

"How does she survive?" I questioned Jo-An. "She'll die of cold."

He frowned. "She is sustained by God. It does not matter to her if she dies."

"She is like you, then?"

"She is a holy person. Once I thought she was an angel, but she is a human being, transformed by the power of God."

He did not want to talk more. He seemed to have caught my urgency. We descended at a rapid pace until we came to a small rockfall, which we clambered over. On the other side was a narrow path made by men walking single file into the dark forest. Once on the path we began to climb again.

Fallen leaves and pine needles muffled our footsteps. Beneath the trees it was almost night. Jo-An went faster still. The pace warmed me a little, but my feet and legs seemed to be slowly turning to stone, as if the limy water I'd drunk were calcifying me. And my heart was chilled, too, by the old woman's baffling words and all that they implied for my future. I had never fought in a battle: Was I really to wage five of them? If bloodshed was the price of peace, in five battles it would be a heavy cost indeed. And the idea that my own son, not yet even born, would be the one to kill me filled me with unbearable sadness.

I caught up with Jo-An and touched him on the arm. "What does it mean?"

"It means what it says," he replied, slowing a little to catch his breath.

"Did she say the same words to you earlier?"

"The same."

"When was it?"

"After I died and came back to life. I wanted to live like her, a hermit on the mountain. I thought I might be her servant, her disciple. But she said my work in the world was not yet finished, and she spoke the words about you."

"You told her who I was, my past life and everything?"

"No," he said patiently. "There was no need to tell her, for she already knew. She said I must serve you, because only you will bring peace."

"Peace?" I repeated. Was this what she meant by heaven's desire? I wasn't even sure what the word signified. The very idea of peace seemed like one of the fantasies of the Hidden, the stories of the kingdom that my mother would whisper to me at night. Would it ever be possible to stop the clans from fighting? The whole warrior class fought: It was what they were bred and trained and lived for. Apart from their traditions and personal sense of honor, there was the constant need for land to maintain armies to gain more land, the military codes and shifting webs of alliances, the overweening ambition of warlords like Iida Sadamu, and now, more than likely, Arai Daiichi. "Peace through war?"

"Is there any other way?" Jo-An replied. "There will be battles."

Four to win, one to lose. . . .

"That is why we are preparing now. You noticed the men at the tannery, saw their eyes. Ever since your merciful actions at Yamagata Castle, when you put an end to the sufferings of the tortured Hidden, you have been a hero to these people. Then your service to Lord Shigeru at Inuyama ... even without the prophecy they would have been ready to fight for you. Now they know God is with you."

"She sits in a mountain shrine and uses a prayer wheel," I said. "Yet, she blessed us after the fashion of your people."

"*Our* people," he corrected me.

I shook my head. "I no longer follow those teachings. I have killed many times. Do you really believe she speaks the words of your god?"

For the Hidden teach that the Secret God is the only true one, and the spirits that everyone else worships are delusions.

"I don't know why God tells me to listen to her," he admitted. "But he does, and so I do."

He is mad, I thought. *The torture and the fear have driven him out of his mind.* "She said, 'It is all one.' But you don't believe that, surely?"

He whispered, "I believe all the teachings of the Secret One. I have followed them since childhood. I know them to be true. But it seems to me there is a place beyond the teachings, a place beyond words, where that could be the truth, where all the beliefs are seen to issue from the one source. My brother was a priest; he would have said this was heresy. I have not been to this place yet, but it is where she dwells."

I was silent, thinking about how his words applied to myself. I could feel the three elements that made up my nature coiled within me like three separate snakes, each one deadly to the others if it were allowed to strike. I could never live one life without denying two-thirds of myself. My only way was to go forward, to transcend the divisions and find a means of uniting them.

"And you also," Jo-An added, reading my thoughts.

"It is what I would like to believe," I said finally. "But whereas for her it is a place of deepest spirituality, I am perhaps more practical. To me it just seems to make sense."

"So you are the one who will bring peace."

I did not want to believe this prophecy. It was both far more and far less than I wanted for my own life. But the old woman's words had fallen into my inner being, and I could not get rid of them.

"The men at the tannery, your men, they won't fight, will they?"

"Some will," Jo-An said.

"Do they know how to?"

"They can be taught. And there are many other things they can do: building, transport, guiding you over secret paths."

"Like this one?"

"Yes, the charcoal burners made this one. They conceal the entrances with rock piles. They have ways over the whole mountain."

Farmers, outcasts, charcoal burners—none of them was supposed to carry weapons or join in the wars of the clans. I wondered how many others were like the farmer I had killed at Matsue, or Jo-An. What a waste of their courage and intelligence not to use men like that. If I were to train and arm them, I would have all the men I needed. But would warriors fight alongside them? Or would they just consider me an outcast, too?

I was occupied with these thoughts when I caught the whiff of burning and a few moments later heard the distant sound of voices, and other noises of human activity, the thud of an ax, the crackle of fire. Jo-An noticed as I swung my head.

"You hear them already?"

I nodded, listening, counting how many there were. Four from the voices, I thought; maybe another who did not speak but who moved with a distinctive tread; no dogs, which seemed unusual. "You know I am half Kikuta, from the Tribe. I have many of their talents."

He couldn't help flinching slightly. These talents seem like witchcraft to the Hidden. My own father had renounced all his Tribe skills when he had converted to the beliefs of the Hidden; he had died because he had taken their vow never to kill again.

"I know it," Jo-An replied.

"I'll need all of them if I'm to do what you expect of me."

"The Tribe are children of the Devil," he muttered, adding quickly as he had once before, "But your case is different, lord."

It made me realize the risks he was taking for me, not only from human forces, but from supernatural ones. My Tribe blood must have made me as dangerous in his mind as a goblin or a river spirit. I was amazed again at the strength of the convictions that drove him and at how completely he had placed himself in my hands.

The smell of burning grew stronger. Flecks of ash were settling on our clothes and skin, reminding me ominously of snow. The ground took on a grayish look. The path led into a clearing between the trees where there were several charcoal ovens, banked over with damp soil and turf. Only one still burned, patches of red glowing from its crevices. Three men were engaged in dismantling the cold ovens and bundling the charcoal. Another knelt by a cooking fire where a kettle hung steaming from a three-legged stand. Four, yet I still felt there had been five. I heard a heavy footfall behind me, and the involuntary intake of breath that precedes an attack. I pushed Jo-An aside and leaped round to face whoever it was trying to ambush us.

He was the largest man I had ever seen, arms already stretched out to seize us. One huge hand, one stump. Because of the stump I hesitated to wound him more. Leaving my image on the path, I slipped behind him and called to him to turn round, holding the knife where he could see the blade clearly and threatening to cut his throat.

Jo-An was shouting, "It's me, you blockhead! It's Jo-An!"

The man by the fire let out a great shout of laughter and the charcoal burners came running.

"Don't hurt him, sir," they called to me. "He doesn't mean any harm. You surprised him, that's all."

The giant had lowered his arms and stood with his one hand held out in a gesture of submission.

"He's mute," Jo-An told me. "But even with one hand he's as strong as two oxen, and he's a hard worker."

The charcoal burners were clearly worried I was going to punish one of their greatest assets. They threw themselves at my feet, begging for mercy. I told them to get up and keep their giant under control.

"I could have killed him!"

They all got up, said the words of welcome, clapped Jo-An on the shoulder, bowed again to me, and made me sit down by the fire. One of them poured tea from the kettle. I had no idea what it was made from; it tasted unlike anything I'd ever had before, but it was hot. Jo-An took them to one side and they had a huddled whispered conversation, of which I could hear every word.

Jo-An told them who I was, which produced gasps and more bowing, and that I had to get to Terayama as soon as possible. The group argued a little about the safest route and whether to start right away or wait till morning, then they came back to the fire, sat in a circle, and stared at me, their eyes glowing in their dark faces. They were covered in soot and ash, barely clothed, yet not noticing the cold. They spoke as a group and seemed to think and feel as one. I imagined that here in the forest they followed their own rules, living like wild men, almost like animals.

"They've never spoken to a lord before," Jo-An said. "One of them wants to know if you are the hero Yoshitsune, returned from the mainland. I told them that though you wander the mountains like Yoshitsune and are pursued by all men, you will be an even greater hero, for he failed but you are promised success by God."

"Will the lord allow us to cut wood where we please?" one of the older men asked. They did not speak to me directly but addressed all their remarks to Jo-An. "There are many parts of the forest where we are no longer allowed to go. If we cut a tree there . . ." He made a graphic gesture of slicing his own neck.

"A head for a tree, a hand for a branch," said another. He reached over to the giant and held up the mutilated arm. The stump had healed over with a puckered, livid scar, traces of gray running back up the limb where it had been cauterized. "Tohan clan officials did this to him a couple of years ago. He didn't understand, but they still took his hand."

The giant held it out to me, nodding several times, his face bewildered and sorrowful.

I knew the Otori clan also had laws forbidding indiscriminate felling of trees: It was to protect the forests forever, but I did not think they enforced such harsh penalties. I wondered what was the point of half crippling a man; was a human life really worth less than a tree's?

"Lord Otori will reclaim all these lands," Jo-An said. "He will rule from sea to sea. He will bring justice."

They bowed again, swearing that they would serve me, and I promised I would do all I could for them when that day came. Then they fed us—meat: small birds they had caught and a hare. I ate meat so rarely I could not remember when I had last tasted it, apart from the wrestlers' chicken stew. That flesh, however, had been bland compared to the hare. They'd trapped it a week ago, saving it for their final night on the mountain, burying it out of the sight of any clan official who might come prying round the camp. It tasted of the earth and of blood.

While we ate they discussed their plans for the following day. They decided one of them would show me the way to the border. They did not dare cross it themselves, but the way down the mountain to Terayama was plain enough, they thought. We would leave at first light and it should take me no more than twelve hours, if the snow held off.

The wind had shifted slightly to the north, and it held a threatening rawness. They had already planned to dismantle the last oven that evening and begin the trek down the mountain the following day. Jo-An could help them if he stayed overnight, standing in for the man who would be my guide.

"They don't object to working with you?" I said to Jo-An later. I was puzzled by the charcoal burners. They ate meat, so they did not follow the teachings of the Enlightened One, they did not pray over their food in the manner of the Hidden, and they accepted the outcast to eat and work alongside, quite unlike the villagers.

"They are also outcasts," he replied. "They burn corpses as well as wood. But they are not of the Hidden. They worship the spirits of the forest, in particular the god of fire. They believe he will travel down the mountain with them tomorrow and dwell with them all winter, keeping their houses warm. In the spring they accompany him back to the mountain." Jo-An's voice held a note of disapproval. "I try to tell them about the Secret God," he said. "But they say they cannot leave their ancestors' god, for who then would light the fire for the ovens?"

"Maybe it's all one," I said, teasing him a little, for the meat and the warmth that the fire god provided had raised my spirits.

He gave me one of his slight smiles but said no more on the subject. He looked suddenly exhausted. The light was almost gone and the charcoal burners invited us into their shelter. It was roughly built from branches and covered with hides, which I guessed they had swapped for charcoal with the tanners. We crawled in with them, all huddled together against the cold. My head, closest to the oven, was warm enough, but my back was icy, and when I turned over I thought my eyelids would freeze shut.

I did not sleep much but lay listening to the deep breathing of the men around me, thinking about my future. I had thought I had placed myself under the death sentence of the Tribe, each day hardly expecting to be still alive at nightfall, but the prophetess had given me back my life. My own skills had developed relatively late: Some of the boys I had trained with in Matsue were already showing signs of talent as young as eight or nine. How old would my son be? How long would it be before he was skilled enough to confront me? Maybe as much as sixteen years; it was nearly my entire lifetime. This bald calculation gave me some bitter hope.

Sometimes I believed in the prophecy and sometimes I did not, and so it has been all my life.

Tomorrow I would be at Terayama. I would have Shigeru's records of the Tribe, I would hold Jato in my hands again. In the spring I would approach Arai. Armed with my secret information on the Tribe, I would seek his support against Shigeru's uncles. For it was obvious to me that my first encounter must be with them. Avenging Shigeru's death and taking up my inheritance would give me what I most needed, a power base in impregnable Hagi.

Jo-An slept restlessly, twitching and whimpering. I realized he was probably always in pain, yet awake he gave no sign of it. Toward dawn the cold eased a little and I slept deeply for about an hour, only to wake with a soft, feathery sound filling my ears, the sound I dreaded. I crawled to the entrance of the shelter. In the firelight I could see the flakes beginning to fall, could hear the tiny hiss as they melted on the embers. I shook Jo-An and woke the charcoal burners.

"It's snowing!"

They leaped up, lit branches for torches, and began to pack up their camp. They had no more desire to be trapped on the mountain than I did. The precious charcoal from the last oven was wrapped in the damp hides off the shelter. They prayed quickly over the embers of the fire and placed them in an iron pot to be carried with them down the mountain.

The snow was still fine and powdery, mostly not settling but melting as soon as it touched the ground. However, as dawn came we could see that the sky was gray and ominous, the clouds full of more snow to come. The wind was picking up, too; when the heavier snow did start to fall, it would be as a blizzard.

There was no time to eat, no time even for tea. Once all the charcoal was ready, the men were eager to get away. Jo-An dropped to his knees before me, but I raised him up and embraced him. His frame in my arms was as bony and frail as an old man's.

"We will meet again in the spring," I said. "I will send word to you at the outcasts' bridge."

He nodded, suddenly overcome with emotion, as though he could not bear to let me out of his sight. One of the men raised a bundle and placed it across his shoulders. The others were already filing down the slope. Jo-An made a clumsy gesture to me, a cross between a farewell and a blessing. Then he turned and, stumbling a little under the weight of the burden, walked away.

I watched him for a moment, finding myself repeating under my breath the familiar words the Hidden use when they part.

"Come, lord," my guide called to me anxiously, and I turned and followed him up the slope.

We climbed for what must have been nearly three hours. My guide paused only to bend twigs now and then to mark the path back. The snow stayed the same, light and dry, but the higher we climbed, the more it settled, until ground and trees all had a thin powdering of white. The rapid climb warmed me, but my stomach was growling with hunger. The meat the night before had given it false expectations. It was impossible to guess the hour. The sky was a uniform brownish gray, and the ground was beginning to give off the strange, disorienting light of a snowy landscape.

When my guide stopped we were halfway up the main peak of the mountain range. The path we'd been following now twisted away downward. I could see the valley below through the veil of falling flakes, the massive branches of the beeches and cedars already turning white.

"Can't go any farther with you," he said. "Want my advice, you turn back with me now. Blizzard's coming. Best part of a day's walk to the temple, even in fair weather. You go on, you perish in the snow."

"It's impossible for me to go back," I replied. "Come a little farther with me. I'll pay you well for it." But I could not persuade him, nor did I really want to. He seemed uneasy and lonely without his fellows. I gave him half the coins I had left anyway, and in return he gave me a leg bone from the hare with a fair bit of meat still attached to it.

He described the path I had to take, pointing out the landmarks across the valley as best he could in the dim light. A river ran through it, he told me, not knowing I'd already heard it long before. This marked the fief boundary. There was no bridge, but at one point it was narrow enough to jump across. The pools beneath held water spirits and the current was swift, so I must be careful not to fall in. Also, as this was the easiest place to cross, sometimes it was patrolled, though he did not think that was likely on such a day as this.

Once into the next fief, I was to continue in an easterly direction, descending toward a small shrine. Here the paths forked. I must take the right-hand, lower path. I had to keep going east, otherwise I would find myself climbing the mountain range. The wind was from the northeast now, so I had to keep it against my left shoulder. He touched my shoulder twice to emphasize this, peering into my face with his narrow eyes.

"You don't look like a lord," he said, his features twisting in a sort of smile. "But good luck to you anyway."

I thanked him and set off down the slope, gnawing the bone as I went, cracking it open with my teeth and sucking out the marrow. The snow became slightly wetter and denser, melting more slowly on my head and clothes. The man was right: I did not look like a lord. My hair, which had not been cut since Yuki had clipped it in the style of an actor, hung shaggy round my ears, and I had not shaved for days. My clothes were soaked and filthy. I certainly did not smell like a lord. I tried to remember when I'd last had a bath—and suddenly recalled the wrestlers' stable, our first night out from Matsue: the vast bathhouse, the conversation I'd overheard between Akio and Hajime.

I wondered where Yuki was now, if she had heard of my defection. I could hardly bear to think about the child. In the light of the prophecy, the idea of my son being kept from me and taught to hate me had become even more painful. I remembered Akio's taunt; it seemed the Kikuta knew my character better than I knew it myself.

The noise of the river grew louder, almost the only sound in the snow-filled landscape. Even the crows were silent. The snow was starting to cap the boulders along the water's edge as I came within sight of it. It fell from the mountain some distance upstream in a waterfall, then spread wide between steep crags, tumbling over rocks in a series of rapids before being forced into a narrow channel between two flat outcrops. Ancient, twisted pines clung to the sides of the crags, and the whole landscape, whitened out by the snow, looked as if it were waiting for Sesshu to come and paint it.

I crouched down behind a boulder where a small pine clung precariously to the thin soil. It was more of a bush than a tree, and it gave me a little shelter. The snow was covering the path, but it was easy enough to see where it led and where to jump across the river. I looked at the crossing for a while, listening intently.

The pattern of the water over the rocks was not quite constant. Every now and then a lull appeared, bringing an uncanny silence, as though I were not the only creature listening. It was easy to imagine spirits dwelling beneath the water, stopping and starting the flow, teasing and provoking humans, luring them to the edge.

I thought I could even hear them breathing. Then, just as I'd isolated the sound, the ripple and babble of the river started up again. It was infuriating. I knew I was wasting time, crouched in a bush being gradually covered by snow, listening to spirits, but slowly the conviction grew that there was someone breathing, not all that far from me.

Just beyond the narrow crossing, the river dropped another ten feet or so into a series of deep pools. I caught a sudden movement and realized a heron, almost completely white, was fishing in one of them, oblivious to the snow. It was like a sign—the Otori emblem on the boundary of the Otori fief—perhaps a message from Shigeru that I had made the right choice at last.

The heron was on the same side of the river as I was, working its way along the pool toward me. I wondered what it found to eat in midwinter, when frogs and toads were hidden away in the mud. It seemed tranquil and unafraid, certain that nothing threatened it in this lonely place. As I watched it, feeling as safe as it did, thinking that at any moment I would walk to the river and jump across, something startled it. It swung its long head toward the shore and instantly launched itself into flight. The clack of its wings sounded once above the water and then it disappeared silently downstream.

What had it seen? I strained my eyes, staring at the same spot. The river fell silent for a moment, and I heard the breathing. I flared my nostrils and on the northeasterly wind caught a faint, human scent. I could see no one; yet, I knew someone was there, lying invisible in the snow.

He was so placed that if I went directly to the crossing, he could easily cut me off. If he could maintain invisibility for as long as he had, he had to be from the Tribe, and so might be able to see me as soon as I approached the river. My only hope was to take him by surprise and jump farther upstream, where the crossing was wider.

There was no point in waiting any longer. I took a deep, silent breath and ran out from the cover of the pine tree and down the slope. I kept to the path as long as I could, not sure of the footing beneath the snow. As I broke away from it toward the river I looked sideways and saw my enemy rise up out of the snow. He was dressed entirely in white. I felt a moment of relief that he had not been invisible, merely camouflaged—maybe he was not from the Tribe; maybe he was just a border guard—then the dark chasm loomed beneath me and I jumped.

The river roared and fell silent, and in the silence I heard something spinning through the air behind me. As I landed I threw myself to the ground, scrabbling on the icy rock, almost losing my grip. The flying object whistled over my head. If I'd been standing it would have caught me in the back of the neck. Before me lay the star-shaped hole it had made in the snow. Only the Tribe use such throwing knives, and they usually use several, one after the other.

I rolled, pulled myself to safety, still keeping low, and went invisible at once. I knew I could maintain invisibility until I reached the shelter of the forest, but I did not know if he could see me or not and I forgot about the tracks I would leave in the snow. Luckily for me, he also slipped as he leaped across the river, and while he looked bigger and heavier than me and could probably run faster, I had a head start on him.

Under the cover of the trees I split myself and sent the

image sideways up the slope while I ran on down the path, knowing that I could not outrun him for long, that my only hope was to ambush him somehow. Ahead, the path curved round a large rocky outcrop; a tree branch hung above it. I ran round the corner, stepped back in my own footprints, and sprang for the branch. I pulled myself up onto it and took out my knife, wishing I had Jato. The other weapons I carried were those with which I'd been meant to kill Ichiro, garrote and neck spike. But the Tribe are hard to kill with their own weapons, just as they are hard to outwit with their own tricks. My best hope was the knife. I stilled my breathing, went invisible, listened to him falter as he saw my second self, then heard him run again.

I knew I would only have one chance. I dropped on him from above. My weight unbalanced him, and as he stumbled I found a gap in his neck protection and drove the knife into the main artery of the throat, pulling it crossways through the windpipe as Kenji had taught me. He made a grunt of amazement—one I've often heard from Tribe members who don't expect to have to play the part of the victim—and the stumble turned into a fall. I slipped from him. His hands went up to his throat, where the breath was whistling noisily and the blood was spurting. Then he went down for good, on his face, the blood turning the snow red.

I went through his clothes and took the rest of the knives and his short sword, which was a particularly fine one. He had a selection of poisons, which I also took, having none of my own at that time. I had no idea who he was. I removed his gloves and looked at his palms, but they did not bear the distinctive straight line of the Kikuta, and as far as I could see he had no tattoos.

I left his body for the crows and foxes, thinking it would be a welcome winter meal for them, and hurried on as quickly and as silently as possible, fearing he might be one of a band watching the river, waiting for me. The blood was racing through me; I was warmed by my flight and the brief struggle, and I was deeply, primitively glad it was not me lying dead in the snow.

I was slightly alarmed that the Tribe had caught up with me so quickly and had known where I would be going. Had Akio's body been discovered, and messages sent already, by horse, from Hagi to Yamagata? Or was Akio still alive? I cursed myself for not taking the time to finish him off. Maybe the encounter should have frightened me more, should have made me realize what it would be like to be hunted by the Tribe for the rest of my life. I did realize it, but I was enraged that they should try to kill me like a dog in the forest and cheered by the fact that their first attempt had failed. The Tribe might have managed to kill my father, but Kenji himself had said no one would have been able to get near him if he had not taken a vow never to kill again. I knew I had all his talents, maybe even more. I would not let the Tribe near me. I would carry on Shigeru's work and break their power.

All these thoughts whirled through my mind as I slogged on through the snow. They gave me energy and sharpened my resolve to survive. After I'd finished with the Tribe, I turned my rage against the Otori lords, whose treachery seemed even greater to me. Warriors pretended that honor and loyalty were all-important to them; yet, their deceptions and betrayals were as deep and as self-serving as the Tribe's. Shigeru's uncles had sent him to his death and were now trying to dispossess me. They did not know what lay in store for them.

If they could have seen me, knee-deep in drifts of snow, ill-clad, ill-equipped, with no men, money, or land, they would certainly have lost no sleep over any threat I posed them.

I could not stop and rest. I had no alternative but to keep walking until I reached Terayama or dropped in my tracks from exhaustion, but every now and then I stepped off the path and listened for any sound of pursuit. I heard nothing except the moan of the wind and the soft hiss of the flakes as they fell, until, late in the day when the light was beginning to fade, I thought I could hear snatches of sound from below.

It was the last thing I would have expected to hear out on the mountain as the forest filled with snow. It sounded like flute music, as lonely as the wind in the pines, as fleeting as the flakes. It sent shivers down my spine, not only from the usual effect music has on me, but from a deeper fear. I believed I had come too close to the edge of the world and was hearing spirits. I thought of the mountain goblins who lure humans and keep them captive below the ground for thousands of years. I wished I could form the prayers my mother taught me, but my lips were frozen, and anyway, I no longer believed in their power.

The music grew louder. I was approaching its source, but I could not stop walking, as though it had enchanted me and was drawing me toward itself. I rounded the corner and saw the path fork. Immediately, I remembered what my guide had told me, and indeed, there was the little shrine, just visible, three oranges placed before it glowing bright beneath their caps of snow. Behind the shrine was a small hut with wooden walls and a thatched roof. My fears subsided at once and I almost laughed aloud. It was no goblin I'd heard but some monk or hermit who had retreated to the mountain to seek enlightenment.

Now I could smell smoke. The warmth drew me irresistibly. I could imagine the coals drying my soaked feet, bringing them back from the blocks of ice they'd turned into. I could almost feel the heat on my face. The door of the hut was open to let light in and smoke out. The flute player had neither heard nor seen me. He was lost in the sorrowful, unearthly music.

Even before I saw him, I knew who he was. I had heard the same music before, night after night as I grieved at Shigeru's grave. It was Makoto, the young monk who had comforted me. He sat cross-legged, his eyes closed. He was playing the long bamboo flute, but a smaller transverse flute lay on the cushion beside him. A brazier burned smokily near the entrance. At the back of the hut was a raised sleeping area. A wooden fighting pole leaned against the wall, but no other weapons were visible. I stepped in—even with the brazier it was only slightly warmer than outside—and said quietly, "Makoto?"

He did not open his eyes or stop playing.

I said his name again. The music faltered and he took the flute from his lips. He spoke in a whisper, wearily: "Leave me alone. Stop tormenting me. I am sorry. I am sorry." He still did not look up.

As he took up the flute again I knelt before him and touched him on the shoulder. He opened his eyes, looked at me, and, taking me completely by surprise, leaped to his feet, throwing the flute aside. He backed away from me, seized the pole, and held it out threateningly. His eyes were filled with suffering, his face gaunt, as though he had been fasting. "Stay away from me," he said, his voice low and hoarse.

I stood, too. "Makoto," I said gently, "it's no enemy. It's me: Otori Takeo."

I took a step toward him and he immediately swung the pole at my shoulder. I saw it coming and deflected it a little, and luckily in the small space he could not swing it hard or he would have broken my collarbone. As it was, he knocked me to the ground. The shock must have reverberated up to his hands, for he dropped the pole and looked at them in astonishment and then at me on the floor.

"Takeo?" he said. "You're real? It's not your ghost?"

"Real enough to half knock out," I said, getting up and flexing my arm. Once I was sure nothing was broken, I reached inside my clothes for my knife. I felt safer with it in my hand.

"Forgive me," he said. "I would never hurt you. It's just that I have seen your apparition so often." He looked as if he would reach out to touch me, then drew back. "I can't believe it's you! What strange fate brings you here at this hour?"

"I am going to Terayama. Twice I've been offered refuge there. Now I need to accept that offer, until spring."

"I can't believe it's you," he repeated. "You're soaked. You must be freezing." He looked round the tiny hut. "I have so little to offer you." He turned toward the sleeping area, tripped over the pole, and bent to retrieve it. Placing it back against the wall, he took one of the thin hempen quilts from the bed. "Take off your clothes. We'll dry them. Wrap yourself in this."

"I must keep going," I said. "I'll just sit by the fire for a while."

"You'll never get to Terayama tonight. It will be dark in an hour, and it's still five hours' walk. Spend the night here; we'll go together in the morning."

"The blizzard will have closed the path by then," I said. "I want to be snowed in at the temple, not snowed out."

"This is the first fall of the year," he replied. "It's heavy on the mountain, but from here downward it is more sleet than snow." He smiled and quoted the old poem: "'On nights when, rain mixing in, the snow falls' . . . unfortunately, I am as poor as the poet and his family!"

It was one of the first pieces Ichiro had taught me to write, and it brought him to my mind with piercing clarity. I was beginning to shiver violently. Now that I was no longer moving, I was indeed freezing. I began to peel off the wet clothes. Makoto took them and stretched them before the brazier, adding a little wood and blowing up the embers.

"This looks like blood," he said. "Are you hurt?"

"No. Someone tried to kill me at the border."

"This blood is his, then?"

I nodded, not sure how much to tell him, for his safety as well as my own.

"Is anyone following you?" he said.

"Either following me or lying in wait for me. That's how it will be for the rest of my life."

"Will you tell me why?" He lit a taper from the fire and held it to the wick of an oil lamp. The lamp spluttered reluctantly into life. "There's not much oil," he apologized, and went to close the outer shutters.

Night stretched before us. "Can I trust you?" I said.

The question made him laugh. "I have no idea what you've been through since we last met, or what brings you to this place now. And you know nothing about me. If you did, you would not need to ask. I'll tell you everything later. In the meantime, yes, you can trust me. If you trust no one else, trust me."

A note of deep emotion had crept into his voice. He turned away. "I'll warm some soup," he said. "I'm sorry, I have neither wine nor tea."

I remembered how he had comforted me in my terrible grief after Shigeru's death. He had reassured me while I was racked by remorse, and had held me until grief had given way to desire, and both had been assuaged.

"I cannot stay with the Tribe," I said. "I've left them, and they will pursue me until they execute me."

Makoto took a pot from the corner of the room and placed it carefully over the embers. He looked toward me again.

"They wanted me to find the records Shigeru kept of them," I said. "They sent me to Hagi. I was supposed to kill Ichiro, my teacher, and give the records to them. But of course they weren't there."

Makoto smiled but still said nothing.

"That is one of the reasons why I have to reach Terayama. Because that's where they are. You knew, didn't you?"

"We would have told you if you had not already chosen to go with the Tribe," he said. "But our duty to Lord Shigeru meant we could not take the risk. He entrusted the records to us, for he knew our temple is one of the few in the Three Countries that has not been infiltrated by Tribe members."

He poured the soup into a bowl and handed it to me. "I only have one bowl. I didn't expect visitors. And the last person I expected was you!"

"Why are you here?" I asked him. "Are you going to spend the winter here?" I didn't voice the thought, but I doubted he would survive. Maybe he didn't want to. I drank a mouthful of soup. It was hot and salty, but that was about

113

all you could say for it. And this seemed to be the only food he had. What had happened to the energetic young man I'd first met at Terayama? What had driven him to this state of resignation, almost despair?

I pulled the quilt around me and edged a little closer to the fire. As always I listened. The wind had strengthened and was whistling through the thatch. Every now and then a gust made the lamp flicker, throwing grotesque shadows onto the opposite wall. The noise of whatever was falling outside was not the soft, breathlike touch of snow but harder and more sleety.

Now that the doors were closed the hut was warming up. My clothes were beginning to steam. I drained the bowl and passed it back to him. He filled it, took a sip, and placed it on the floor.

"The winter, the rest of my life, whichever turns out to be the longer," he said, looked at me, looked down. "It's hard for me to talk to you, Takeo, since so much of it concerns you, but the Enlightened One has seen fit to bring you here, so I have to try. Your presence changes everything. I told you, your apparition has been constantly with me; you visit me at night in dreams. I have been striving to overcome this obsession."

He smiled self-mockingly. "Since I was a child I have tried to practice detachment from the world of the senses. My only desire was enlightenment. I craved holiness. I'm not saying I'd never had attachments: You know what it's like when men live together without women. Terayama is no exception. But I never fell in love with anyone. I never became obsessed as I did with you." Again the smile curved his lips. "I won't go into why. It's not important, and anyway, I'm not sure I even know. However, after Lord Shigeru's death, you were out of your mind with grief. I was moved by your suffering. I wanted to comfort you."

"You did comfort me," I said, in a low voice.

"For me it went beyond comfort! I didn't realize it would be so powerful. I loved the way I felt and was grateful for experiencing what I'd never felt before, and I loathed it. It made all my spiritual strivings seem like a hollow sham. I went to our abbot and told him I thought I should leave the temple and return to the world. He suggested I go away for a while to think about my decision. I have a boyhood friend in the West, Mamoru, who had been pleading with me to visit him. You know, I play the flute a little. I was invited to join Mamoru and others in presenting a drama, *Atsumori*."

He fell silent. The wind threw a flurry of sleet against the wall. The lamp guttered so violently, it almost went out. I had no idea what Makoto was going to say next, but my heart had picked up speed and I could feel the pulse quickening in my throat. Not with desire, though the memory of desire was there; it was more a fear of hearing what I did not want to hear.

Makoto said, "My friend lives in the household of Lord Fujiwara."

I shook my head. I'd never heard of him.

"He is a nobleman living in exile from the capital. His lands run alongside the Shirakawa."

Just to hear her name spoken was like being hit in the belly. "Did you see Lady Shirakawa?"

He nodded.

"I was told she was dying." My heart was hammering so hard, I thought it would leap from my throat.

"She was gravely ill but she recovered. Lord Fujiwara's physician saved her life."

"She's alive?" The dim lamp seemed to brighten until the hut was full of light. "Kaede is alive?"

He studied my face, his own filled with pain. "Yes, and I

am profoundly thankful, for if she had died it would have been me who dealt the fatal blow."

I was frowning, trying to puzzle out his words. "What happened?"

"The Fujiwara household knew her as Lady Otori. It was believed that Lord Shigeru married her secretly at Terayama, on the day he came to his brother's grave, the day we met. I had not expected to see her in Lord Fujiwara's house; I had not been told of her marriage. I was completely taken aback when she was introduced to me. I assumed you had married her—that you were there yourself. I blurted out as much. Not only did I reveal to myself the strength and nature of my obsession with you, which I'd fooled myself I was recovering from, I destroyed her pretense in an instant, in the presence of her father."

"But why would she claim such a thing?"

"Why does any woman claim to be married when she is not? She nearly died because she miscarried a child."

I could not speak.

Makoto said, "Her father questioned me about the marriage. I knew it had not taken place at Terayama. I tried to avoid answering him directly, but he already had his own suspicions and I had said enough to confirm them. I did not know it then, but his mind was very unstable and he had often spoken of taking his own life. He slit his belly in her presence, and the shock must have caused the miscarriage."

I said, "The child was mine. She should have been my wife. She will be."

But as I heard my own words, my betrayal of Kaede seemed all the more enormous. Would she ever forgive me?

"So I assumed," he said. "But when? What were you thinking of? A woman of her rank and family?"

"We were thinking of death. It was the night Shigeru died and Inuyama fell. We did not want to die without . . ." I was unable to continue.

After a few moments Makoto went on, "I could not live with myself. My passion had led me deeply back into the world of suffering I thought I could escape. I felt I had done irreparable harm to another sentient being, even though only a woman, but at the same time some jealous part of me wanted her to die, because I knew that you loved her and that she must have loved you. You see, I am hiding nothing from you. I must tell you the worst about myself."

"I would be the last to condemn you. My own conduct has been far more cruel in its effects."

"But you belong to this world, Takeo; you live in the midst of it. I wanted to be different. Even that was revealed to me as the most hideous pride. I returned to Terayama and sought our abbot's permission to retire to this small hut, where I would devote my flute playing and any passion that remained in me to serving the Enlightened One, though I no longer even hope for his enlightenment, for I am completely unworthy of it."

"We all live in the midst of the world," I said. "Where else is there to live?" As I spoke I thought I heard Shigeru's voice: *Just as the river is always at the door, so is the world always outside. And it is in the world that we have to live.*

Makoto was staring at me, his face suddenly open, his eyes brighter. "Is that the message I am to hear? Is that why you were sent to me?"

"I hardly know my plans for my own life," I replied. "How can I fathom yours? But this was one of the first things I learned from Shigeru. It is in the world that we have to live."

"Then let's take it as a command from him," Makoto

said, and I could see the energy beginning to flow back into him. He seemed to have been resigned to death, but now he was coming back to life before my eyes. "You intend now to carry out his wishes?"

"Ichiro told me I must take revenge on Shigeru's uncles and claim my inheritance, and so I mean to. But as to how I achieve it, I have no idea. And I must marry Lady Shirakawa. That was also Shigeru's desire."

"Lord Fujiwara wishes to marry her," Makoto said carefully.

I wanted to brush this aside. I could not believe Kaede would marry anyone else. Her last words to me had been, "I will never love anyone but you." And before that she had said, "I am only safe with you." I knew the reputation she had acquired: that any man who touched her died. I had lain with her and lived. I had given her a child. And I had abandoned her, she had nearly died, she had lost our child. . . . Would she ever forgive me?

Makoto went on: "Fujiwara prefers men to women. But he seems to have become obsessed with Lady Shirakawa. He proposes a marriage in name only, to give her his protection. Presumably he is also not indifferent to her inheritance. Shirakawa is pitifully run-down, but there is always Maruyama."

When I made no comment he murmured, "He is a collector. She will become one of his possessions. His collection never sees the light of day. It is shown only to a few privileged friends."

"That cannot happen to her!"

"What other choices does she have? She is lucky not to be completely disgraced. To have survived the deaths of so many men connected with her is shameful enough. But there is also something unnatural about her. They say she had two of her father's retainers put to death when they would not serve her. She reads and writes like a man. And apparently she is raising an army to claim Maruyama for herself in the spring."

"Maybe she will be her own protection," I said.

"A woman?" Makoto replied, scornful. "It's impossible."

I felt my heart swell with admiration for Kaede. What an ally she would make! If we were to marry, we would hold half the Seishuu territory. Maruyama would give me all the resources I needed to fight the Otori lords. Once they were dealt with, only the former Tohan heartland which was now

Arai's, would prevent our lands from stretching from sea to sea as the prophecy promised.

Now that the snows had begun, everything had to wait till spring. I was exhausted; yet, I burned with impatience. I dreaded Kaede making an irrevocable decision before I saw her again.

"You said you would go with me to the temple?"

Makoto nodded. "We'll leave as soon as it's light."

"But you would have stayed here all winter if I had not stumbled in on you?"

"I have no illusions," he replied. "I would probably have died here. Maybe you have saved my life."

We talked until late into the night. Makoto talked as if the presence of another human being had unlocked weeks of silence. He told me something of his background; he was four years older than I was and had been born into a low-ranking warrior family that had served the Otori until Yaegahara and after that defeat had been forced to transfer their allegiance to the Tohan. He had been brought up as a warrior but was the fifth son in a large family that became steadily more impoverished. From an early age his love of learning and his interest in religion had been encouraged, and when the family began its decline, he had been sent to Terayama. He was eleven years old. His brother, then thirteen, had also been intended as a novice, but after the first winter he had run away and had not been heard of since. The oldest brother had been killed at Yaegahara; their father died not long after. His two sisters were married to Tohan warriors, and he had heard nothing from them for years. His mother still lived on the family farm, such as it was, with his two surviving brothers and their families. They hardly considered themselves as part of the warrior class anymore. He saw his mother once or twice a year.

We talked easily, like old friends, and I remembered how I had longed for such a companion when I was on the road with Akio. A little older and much better educated than I was, Makoto had a gravity and thoughtfulness that contrasted with my reckless nature. Yet, as I was to find out later, he was both strong and courageous, still a warrior as well as a monk and a scholar.

He went on to tell me about the horror and outrage that swept through Yamagata and Terayama after Shigeru's death.

"We were armed and prepared for an uprising. Iida had been threatening the destruction of our temple for some time, aware that we were growing richer and more powerful every year. He knew what strong resentment there was about being ceded to the Tohan, and he hoped to nip any rebellion in the bud. You saw how the people regarded Lord Shigeru. Their sense of loss and grief at his death was terrible. I'd never seen anything like it. The riots in the town that the Tohan had feared while he lived erupted with even more violence at the news of his death. There was a spontaneous uprising; former Otori warriors, townspeople armed with stakes, even farmers with scythes and stones, advanced on the castle. We were poised to join the attack when news came of Iida's death and Arai's victory at Inuyama. The Tohan forces fell back, and we began to chase them toward Kushimoto.

"We met you on the road, with Iida's head. By then everyone was beginning to know the story about your rescue of Lord Shigeru. And they began to guess the identity of the one they called the Angel of Yamagata."

He sighed and blew on the last of the embers. The lamp had long since gone out. "When we returned to Terayama, you did not seem like a hero at all. You were as lost and grief-stricken as anyone I'd ever seen and still faced with heartrending decisions. You interested me when we first met, but I thought you strange—talented maybe but weak; your sense of hearing seemed freakish, like an animal's. Usually I consider myself a good judge of men. I was surprised when you were given an invitation to come back again, and puzzled by Shigeru's confidence in you. I realized you were not what you seemed, saw what courage you must have had, and glimpsed the strength of your emotions. I fell in love with you. As I said, it had never happened to me before. And I said I wasn't going to tell you why, but now I have."

After a moment he added, "I won't speak of it again."

"There's no harm," I replied. "The opposite, rather. I need friendship more than anything else in the world."

"Apart from an army?"

"That has to wait till spring."

"I'll do anything in my power to help you."

"What about your calling, your search for enlightenment?"

"Your cause is my calling," he said. "Why else would the Enlightened One bring you here to remind me that we live in the midst of the world? A bond of great strength exists between us. And I see now that I don't have to struggle against it."

The fire was almost out. I could no longer see Makoto's face. Beneath the thin quilt I was shivering. I wondered if I could sleep, would ever sleep again, would ever stop listening for the assassin's breath. In a world that seemed almost entirely hostile, Makoto's devotion touched me deeply. I could think of nothing to say. I took his hand and clasped it briefly in thanks.

"Will you keep watch while I sleep for a couple of hours?"

"Of course I will."

"Wake me, and then you can sleep before we go."

He nodded. I wrapped myself in the second quilt and lay down. The faintest glow came from the fire. I could hear its dying susurration. Outside the wind had dropped a little. The eaves dripped; some small creature was rustling in the thatch. An owl hooted and the mouse went still. I drifted into an uneasy sleep and dreamed of children drowning. I plunged again and again into icy black water but was unable to save them.

The cold woke me. Dawn was just beginning to lighten the hut. Makoto sat in the position of meditation. His breathing was so slow, I could hardly hear it; yet, I knew he was completely alert. I watched him for a few moments. When he opened his eyes I looked away.

"You should have woken me."

"I feel rested. I need very little sleep." He said curiously, "Why don't you ever look at me?"

"I might send you to sleep. It's one of the Tribe skills I inherited. I should be able to control it, but I've put people to sleep without meaning to. So I don't look them in the eye."

"You mean there's more than just the hearing? What else?"

"I can make myself invisible—for long enough to confuse an opponent or slip past a guard. And I can seem to remain in a place after I've left it or to be in two places at once. We call it using the second self." I watched him without appearing to as I said this, for I was interested in his reaction.

He could not help recoiling slightly. "Sounds more like a demon than an angel," he muttered. "Can all these people, the Tribe, do this?"

"Different people have different skills. I seem to have inherited many more than my share."

"I knew nothing about the Tribe, did not even know they existed, until our abbot spoke of you and your connection with them, after your visit in the summer."

"Many think the skills are sorcery," I said.

"Are they?"

"I don't know, because I don't know how I do them. The skills came to me. I did not seek them. But training enhances them."

"I suppose like any skills they can be used for good or evil," he said quietly.

"Well, the Tribe want only to use them for their own purposes," I said. "Which is why they will not let me live. If you come with me, you will be in the same danger. Are you prepared for that?"

He nodded. "Yes, I'm prepared. Doesn't it alarm you, though? It would make most men weak with fear."

I did not know how to answer. I have often been described as fearless, but that seems too fine a word for a state that is more like invisibility, a gift I was born with. And fearlessness only comes on me from time to time, and then takes energy to maintain. I know fear as well as any man. I didn't want to think about it then. I stood and took up my clothes. They were not really dry, and they felt clammy against my skin as I put them on. I went outside to piss. The air was raw and damp, but the snow had stopped, and what lay on the ground was slushy. There were no footprints around the hut and shrine save my own, already half-covered. The track disappeared downhill. It was passable. The mountain and the forest were silent, apart from the wind. Far in the distance I could hear crows, and a little closer some smaller bird piped in a mournful way. I could hear no sound of human existence, no ax on trunk, no temple bell, no village dog. The shrine spring made a low, welling sound. I washed my face and hands in the icy black water and drank deeply.

That was all the breakfast we had. Makoto packed his few possessions, tucked the flutes into his belt, and picked up the fighting pole. It was his only weapon. I gave him the short sword I'd taken from my assailant the day before, and he placed it next to the flutes in his belt.

As we set out, a few flakes of snow were drifting down, and they continued to fall all morning. The path, however, was not too thickly covered, and Makoto of course knew the way well. Every now and then I slipped on an icy patch or stepped in a hole up to my knees. Soon my clothes were as wet as they'd been the night before. The path was narrow; we went in single file at a fair pace, hardly speaking. Makoto seemed to have no words left, and I was too busy listening—

for the breath, the broken stick, the thrum of bowstring, the whistle of throwing knife. I felt like a wild animal, always in danger, always hunted.

The light paled to pearl gray, stayed like that for three hours or so, then began to darken. The flakes fell more heavily, beginning to swirl and settle. Around noon we stopped to drink from a small stream, but as soon as we stopped walking the cold attacked us, so we did not linger.

"This is the North River, which flows past the temple," Makoto said. "We follow its course all the way. It's less than two hours now."

It seemed so much easier than my journey since I'd left Hagi. I almost began to relax. Terayama was only two hours away. I had a companion. We were going to get to the temple, and I would be safe for the winter. But the babbling of the river drowned out all other sound, and so I had no warning of the men who were waiting for us.

There were two of them, and they came at us out of the forest like wolves. But they were anticipating one man—me—and Makoto's presence surprised them. They saw what they thought was a harmless monk and went for him first, expecting him to run away. He dropped the first man with a blow to the head that must have cracked the skull. The second man had a long sword, which surprised me, as the Tribe do not usually carry them. I went invisible as he swung at me, came up under his reach, and slashed at his sword hand, trying to disable him. The knife glanced off his glove. I stabbed again and let my image appear at his feet. The second stab went home, and blood began to drip from his right wrist as he swung again. My second self faded and I, still invisible, leaped on him, trying to slash him in the throat, wishing I had Jato and could fight him properly. He could not see me, but he grabbed at my arms and cried out in horror. I felt myself becoming visible, and he realized it at the same time. He stared into my face as if he saw a ghost, his eyes widening in terror and then beginning to waver, as Makoto struck him from behind, cracking the pole against his neck. He went down like an ox, taking me down with him.

I scrambled out from beneath him and pulled Makoto into the shelter of the rocks, in case there were more of them on the hillside. What I feared most were bowmen who could pick us off from afar. But the forest grew too thickly here to be able to use a bow from any distance. There was no sign of anyone else.

Makoto was breathing hard, his eyes bright. "I realize now what you meant about your skills."

"You're pretty skillful yourself! Thanks."

"Who are they?"

I went to the two bodies. The first man was Kikuta—I could tell from his hands—but the second wore the Otori crest under his armor.

"This one is a warrior," I said, gazing at the heron. "That explains the sword. The other is from the Tribe—Kikuta."

I did not know the man, but we had to be relatives, linked by the lines on our palms.

The Otori warrior made me nervous. Had he come from Hagi? What was he doing with one of the Tribe's assassins? It seemed to be common knowledge that I was heading for Terayama. My thoughts flew to Ichiro. I prayed they had not extracted the information from him. Or was it Jo-An or one of the impoverished men I'd feared would betray me? Maybe these men had already been to the temple and there would be more of them waiting for us there.

"You completely disappeared," Makoto said. "I could only see your prints in the snow. It's extraordinary." He grinned at me, his face transformed. It was hard to believe he was the same person as the despairing flute player of the previous night. "It's been a while since I've had a decent fight. It's amazing how a brush with death makes life so beautiful."

The snow seemed whiter and the cold more piercing. I was terribly hungry, yearning for the comforts of the senses, a scalding bath, food, wine, a lover's body naked against mine.

We went on with renewed energy. We needed it; in the last hour or so the wind increased and the snow began to fall heavily again. I had reason to become even more grateful to Makoto, for by the end we were walking blind; yet he knew the path and never faltered. Since I had last been to the temple, a wooden wall had been erected around the main buildings, and at the gate guards challenged us. Makoto replied and they welcomed him excitedly. They had been anxious for him and were relieved that he had decided to return.

After they had barred the gate again and we were inside the guardroom, they looked searchingly at me, not sure if they knew me or not. Makoto said, "Lord Otori Takeo is seeking refuge here for the winter. Will you inform our abbot that he is here?"

One of them hurried away across the courtyard, his

figure, bowed against the wind, turning white before he reached the cloister. The great roofs of the main halls were already capped with snow, the bare branches of cherry and plum trees heavy with the blossom of winter.

The guards beckoned us to sit by the fire. Like Makoto, they were young monks, their weapons bows, spears, and poles. They poured us tea. Nothing had ever tasted quite as good to me. The tea and our clothes steamed together, creating a comforting warmth. I tried to fight it; I did not want to relax yet.

"Has anyone come here looking for me?"

"Strangers were noticed on the mountain early this morning. They skirted the temple and went on up into the forest. We had no idea they were looking for you. We were a little concerned for Makoto—we thought they might be bandits—but the weather was too bad to send anyone out. Lord Otori has arrived at a good time. The way you came down is already impassable. The temple will be closed now till spring."

"It is an honor for us that you have returned," one of them said shyly, and the glances they exchanged told me they had a fair idea of the significance of my appearance.

After ten minutes or so the monk came hurrying back. "Our abbot welcomes Lord Otori," he said, "and asks that you will bathe and eat. He would like to speak with you when the evening prayers are finished."

Makoto finished his tea, bowed formally to me, and said he must get ready for evening prayers, as though he had spent the whole day in the temple with the other monks, not slogging through a blizzard and killing two men. His manner was cool and formal. I knew beneath it lay the heart of a true friend, but here he was one of the monks, while I had to relearn how to be a lord. The wind howled around the gables; the snow drifted relentlessly down. I had come in safety to Terayama. The winter was mine to reshape my life.

I was taken to one of the temple guest rooms by the young man who'd brought the abbot's message. In spring and summer these rooms would have been full of visitors and pilgrims, but now they were deserted. Even though the outer shutters were closed against the storm, it was bitterly cold. The wind moaned through the chinks in the wall, and through some of the larger ones snow drifted. The same monk showed me the way to the small bathhouse built above a hot spring. I took off my wet, filthy clothes and scrubbed myself all over. Then I eased my body into the hot water. It was even better than I'd imagined it would be. I thought of the men who had tried to kill me in the last two days and was fiercely glad I was alive. The water steamed and bubbled around me. I felt a rush of gratitude for it, that it should well up out of the mountain, bathe my aching body, and unthaw my frozen limbs. I thought about mountains, which were just as likely to spit out ash and fire or shake their sides and throw buildings around like kindling, and make men feel as helpless as the insects that crawl from burning logs. This mountain could have gripped me and frozen me to death, but instead it had given me this scalding water.

My arms were bruised from the warrior's grip, and there was a long, shallow cut on my neck where his sword must have grazed me. My right wrist, which had bothered me on and off ever since Akio had bent it backward, in Inuyama, tearing the tendons, now felt stronger. My body seemed more spare than ever, but otherwise I was in good shape after the journey. And now I was clean too.

I heard footsteps in the room beyond, and the monk called out that he had brought dry clothes and some food. I emerged from the water, my skin bright red from the heat, rubbed myself dry on the rags left there for that purpose, and ran back along the boardwalk through the snow to the room.

It was empty. The clothes lay on the floor: clean loincloth, quilted undergarments, silken outer robe, also quilted, and sash. The robe was a dark plum color woven with a deeper pattern of purple, the Otori crest in silver on the back. I put it on slowly, relishing the touch of the silk. It had been a long time since I had worn anything of this quality. I wondered why it was at the temple and who had left it here. Had it been Shigeru's? I felt his presence envelop me. The first thing I would do in the morning would be to visit his grave. He would tell me how to achieve revenge.

The smell of the food made me realize how famished I was. The meal was more substantial than anything I'd had for days, and it took me just two minutes to devour it. Then, not wanting to lose the heat from the bath or to fall asleep, I went through some exercises, ending with meditation.

Beyond the wind and the snow I could hear the monks chanting from the main hall of the temple. The snowy night, the deserted room with its memories and ghosts, the serene words of the ancient sutras, all combined to produce an exquisite bittersweet sensation. My spine chilled. I wished I could express it, wished I had paid more attention when Ichiro had tried to teach me poetry. I longed to hold the brush in my hand: If I could not express my feelings in words, perhaps I could paint them.

"Come back to us," the old priest had said, "When all this is over . . ." Part of me wished I could do that and spend the rest of my days in this tranquil place. But I remembered how even here I had overheard plans of war; the monks were armed and the temple fortified now. It was far from over; indeed it was only just begun.

The chanting came to an end and I heard the soft pad of feet as the monks filed away to eat, then sleep for a few hours until the bell roused them at midnight. Footsteps approached the room from the cloister, and the same monk came to the door and slid it open. He bowed to me and said, "Lord Otori, our abbot wishes to see you now."

I stood and followed him along the cloister. "What's your name?"

"Norio, sir," he replied, and added in a whisper, "I was born in Hagi."

He did not say more, the rule of the temple being that no one spoke unnecessarily. We walked around the central courtyard, already filled with snow, past the eating hall, where the monks knelt in silent rows, each with a bowl of food in front of him, past the main hall, which smelled of incense and candle wax and where the golden figure sat gleaming in the dimness, to the third side of the square. Here lay a series of small rooms used as offices and studies. From the farthest I could hear the click of prayer beads, the whisper of a sutra. We stopped outside the first room and Norio called in a low voice, "Lord Abbot, your visitor is here."

I was ashamed when I saw him, for it was the old priest himself, in the same old clothes I had seen him in when I had last been at Terayama. I had thought him one of the old men of the temple, not its head. I had been so wrapped up in my own concerns, I had not even known who he was. I dropped to my knees and touched my forehead to the matting. As informal as ever, he came toward me, told me to sit up, and embraced me. Then he sat back and studied me, his face illuminated by his smile. I smiled back, sensing his genuine pleasure and responding to it.

"Lord Otori," he said, "I am very glad you have returned to us safely. You have been much on my mind. You have been through dark times."

"They are not over. But I seek your hospitality for the winter. I seem to be hunted by everyone, and I need a place of safety while I prepare myself."

"Makoto has told me a little of your situation. You are always welcome here."

"I must tell you my purpose right away. I mean to claim my inheritance from the Otori and punish those responsible for Lord Shigeru's death. It may place the temple in some danger."

"We are prepared for that," he replied serenely.

"You are doing me a great kindness that I don't deserve."

"I think you will find that those of us who have long-standing connections with the Otori consider ourselves in your debt," he replied. "And of course we have faith in your future."

More than I have, I thought silently. I felt the color come to my face. It was unthinkable that he should praise me, after all the mistakes I had made. I felt like an impostor, dressed in the Otori robe, with my hair cropped, no money, no possessions, no men, no sword.

"All endeavors start with a single action," he said, as though he could read my mind. "Your first action was to come here."

"My teacher, Ichiro, sent me. He will meet me here in the spring. He advised me to seek Lord Arai's protection. I should have done that from the start."

The abbot's eyes crinkled as he smiled. "No, the Tribe would not have let you live. You were far more vulnerable then. You did not know your enemy. Now you have some inkling of their power."

"How much do you know about them?"

"Shigeru confided in me and sought my advice often. On his last visit we spoke at length about you."

"I didn't hear that."

"No, he was careful to speak by the waterfall so you would not hear. Later we moved into this room."

"Where you spoke of war."

"He needed my assurance that the temple and the town would rise once Iida was dead. He was still of two minds about the assassination attempt, fearing he would simply be sending you to certain death. As it turned out, it was his own death that sparked the uprising, and we could not have prevented it even if we had wanted to. However, Arai was in alliance with Shigeru, not with the Otori clan. If he can take this territory for himself, he will. They will be at war by the summer."

He was silent for a moment, then went on, "The Otori intend to claim Shigeru's land and declare your adoption illegal. Not content with conspiring in his death, they insult his memory. That's why I'm glad you intend to take up your inheritance."

"Will the Otori ever accept me, though?" I held out my hands, palms upward. "I am marked as Kikuta."

"We'll talk about that later. You'll be surprised how many are awaiting your return. You'll see in the spring. Your men will find you."

"An Otori warrior already tried to kill me," I said, unconvinced.

"Makoto told me. The clan will be split, but Shigeru knew this and accepted it. The rift was not of his making: The seeds were sown when he was usurped after his father's death."

"I hold Shigeru's uncles responsible for his death," I said. "But the more I learn, the more it surprises me that they let him live so long."

"Fate decrees the lengths of all our lives," he replied. "The Otori lords fear their own people. Their farmers are volatile by nature and tradition. They have never been completely cowed, like the peasants under the Tohan. Shigeru knew them and respected them and in turn won their respect and affection. That protected him against his uncles. Their loyalty will be transferred to you."

"Maybe," I said, "but there is a more serious problem. I am now sentenced to death by the Tribe."

His face was calm, ivory-colored in the lamplight. "Which I imagine is another reason you are here."

I thought he would go on, but he fell silent. He was watching me with an expectant look on his face.

"Lord Shigeru kept records," I said, speaking carefully into the hushed room. "Records of the Tribe and their activities. I am hoping you will make them available to me."

"They have been kept here for you," he replied. "I will send for them now. And of course there is something else I have been keeping for you."

"Jato," I said.

He nodded. "You are going to need it."

He called to Norio and asked him to go to the storehouse and fetch the chest and the sword.

"Shigeru did not want to influence any decision you might make," he said as I listened to Norio's footsteps echoing away around the cloister. "He was aware that your inheritance would cause divisions in your loyalty. He was quite prepared for you to choose your Kikuta side. In that case no one would ever have access to the records except myself. But since you have chosen your Otori side, the records are yours."

"I have bought myself a few months of life," I said with a trace of self-contempt. "There's no nobility in my choice unless it is that I am finally doing what Lord Shigeru wanted. It's hardly even a choice, since my life with the Tribe was approaching an end. As for my Otori side, it is only by adoption and will be questioned by everyone."

Again the smile lit his face, his eyes bright with understanding and wisdom. "Shigeru's will is as good a reason as any."

I felt he had some other knowledge that he would share with me later, but even as that thought came I heard footsteps returning. I could not help tensing before I recognized them as Norio's, slightly heavier this time: He was carrying the chest and the sword. He slid open the door and stepped inside, dropping to his knees. He placed the chest and the sword on the matting. I did not turn my head, but I heard the soft sound they made. My pulse quickened, with a mixture of joy and fear, at the prospect of holding Jato again.

Norio closed the door behind him and, kneeling again, placed the precious objects in front of the abbot where I, too, could see them. They were both wrapped in pieces of old cloth, their power disguised. The abbot took Jato from its covering and held it out toward me in both hands. I took it in the same fashion, raised it above my head, and bowed to him, feeling the cool familiar weight of the scabbard. I longed to draw the sword and wake its steel song, but I would not do so in the presence of the abbot. I placed it reverently on the floor next to me while he unwrapped the chest.

A smell of rue rose from it. I recognized it at once. It was indeed the one I had carried under Kenji's eyes up the mountain path, thinking it some gift for the temple. Had Kenji no idea then of what it contained?

The old man opened the lid—it was not locked—and the smell of rue intensified. He lifted one of the scrolls and held it out to me.

"You were to read this one first. That was Shigeru's instruction to me." As I took it he said with sudden profound emotion, "I did not think this moment would come."

I looked into his eyes. Deep-set in his old face, they were as bright and as lively as a twenty-year-old's. He held my gaze, and I knew he would never succumb to the Kikuta sleep. In the distance one of the smaller bells rang three times. In my mind's eye I could see the monks at prayer, in meditation. I felt the spiritual power of this holy place, concentrated and reflected in the person of the old man before me now. Again I felt a rush of gratitude—to him, to the belief that sustained him, to heaven, and to the different gods who, despite my own disbelief, seemed to have taken my life into their charge and care.

"Read it," he prompted me. "The rest you can study later, but read this one now."

I unrolled the scroll, frowning at the script. I recognized Shigeru's hand and I knew the characters, my own name among them, but the words made no sense to me. My eyes darted up and down the columns; I unrolled a little more and found myself in a sea of names. It seemed to be a genealogy, like the ones Gosaburo had explained to me in Matsue. Once I'd grasped that, I began to work it out. I went back to the introductory writing and read it carefully again. Then I read it a third time. I looked up at the abbot.

"Is it true?"

He chuckled softly. "It seems it is. You do not see your own face, so you don't see the proof there. Your hands may be Kikuta, but your features are all Otori. Your father's mother worked as a spy for the Tribe. She was employed by the Tohan and sent to Hagi when Shigeru's father, Shigemori, was hardly more than a boy. A liaison occurred, apparently not one sanctioned by the Tribe. Your father was the result. Your grandmother must have been a woman of some ingenuity: She told no one. She was married to one of her cousins and the child was brought up as Kikuta."

"Shigeru and my father were brothers? He was my uncle?"

"It would be hard for anyone to deny it, given the way you look. When Shigeru first set eyes on you, he was struck by your resemblance to his younger brother, Takeshi. Of course, the two brothers were very alike. Now, if your hair were longer, you would be the image of Shigeru as a young man."

"How did he discover this?"

"Some of it from his own family records. His father had always suspected that the woman had conceived a child and confided this to him before he died. The rest Shigeru worked out for himself. He traced your father to Mino and realized a son had been born after his death. Your father must have suffered some of the same conflict as you. Despite being raised as Kikuta and despite his skills, high even by the standards of the Tribe, he still tried to escape from them; in itself this suggests that his blood was mixed and that he lacked the fanaticism of the true Tribe. Shigeru had been compiling his records of the Tribe since he first became acquainted with Muto Kenji. They met at Yaegahara; Kenji was caught up in the fighting and witnessed Shigemori's death." He glanced down at Jato. "He retrieved this sword and gave it to Shigeru. They may have told you the story."

"Kenji once alluded to it," I said.

"Kenji helped Shigeru escape from Iida's soldiers. They were both young men then; they became friends. Apart from the friendship they were useful to each other. Over the years they exchanged information about many things—sometimes, it must be said, unwittingly. I don't believe even Kenji realized how secretive, even devious, Lord Shigeru could be."

I was silent. The revelation had astonished me; yet, on reflection it made perfect sense. It had been my Otori blood that had been so eager to learn the lessons of revenge when my family were massacred at Mino—that same blood that had formed the bond with Shigeru. I grieved for him anew, wished I had known earlier, yet rejoiced that he and I shared the same lineage, that I truly belonged to the Otori.

"This confirms that I have made the right choice," I said finally, in a voice choked by emotion. "But if I am to be one of the Otori, a warrior, I have so much to learn." I gestured at the scrolls in the chest. "Even my reading is poor!"

"You have the whole winter ahead of you," the abbot replied. "Makoto will help you with reading and writing. In the spring you should go to Arai to learn the practice of war. In the meantime you must study its theory and keep up your training with the sword."

He paused and smiled again. I could tell he had another of his surprises in store for me.

"I shall teach you," he said. "Before I was called to the service of the Enlightened One, I was considered something of an expert in these matters. My name in the world was Matsuda Shingen."

Even I had heard this name. Matsuda was one of the most illustrious Otori warriors of the previous generation, a hero to the young men of Hagi. The abbot chuckled as he read the astonishment on my face.

"I think we will enjoy the winter. Plenty of exercise to keep us warm. Take your possessions, Lord Otori. We will begin in the morning. When you are not studying, you will join the monks in meditation. Makoto will rouse you at the hour of the Tiger."

I bowed before him, overwhelmed by gratitude. He waved me away.

"We are just repaying our debt to you."

"No," I said. "I am forever in your debt. I will do anything you tell me. I am completely at your service."

I was at the door when he called out, "Maybe there is one thing."

Turning, I fell to my knees. "Anything!"

"Grow your hair!" he said, laughing.

I could still hear him chuckling as I followed Norio back to the guest room. He was carrying the chest for me, but I held Jato. The wind had dropped a little; the snow had grown wetter and heavier. It dulled sound, blanketing the mountain, shutting off the temple from the world.

In the room the bedding had already been laid out. I thanked Norio and bade him good night. Two lamps lit the room. I drew Jato from its scabbard and gazed on the blade, thinking of the fire that had forged it into this combination of delicacy, strength, and lethal sharpness. The folds in the steel gave it a beautiful wavelike pattern. It was Shigeru's gift to me, along with my name and my life. I held the sword in both hands and went through the ancient movements he had taught me in Hagi.

Jato sang to me of blood and war.

· 3 ·

Kaede came back from afar, out of a red landscape, lapped by fire and blood. She had seen terrifying images during her fever; now she opened her eyes on the familiar light and shade of her parents' house. Often, when she had been a hostage with the Noguchi, she had had this dream of waking at home, only to wake properly a few moments later to the reality of life in the castle. She lay still now, eyes closed, waiting for the second waking, aware of something pricking her in the lower part of her belly and wondering why she should dream of the smell of mugwort.

"She has returned to us!" The man's voice, a stranger's,

startled her. She felt a hand on her brow and knew it was Shizuka's, remembering feeling it there many times before, when its firm, cool shape was the only thing that came between her mind and the terrors that assailed her. It seemed to be all she could remember. Something had happened to her, but her mind shied away from thinking about it. The movement reminded her of falling. She must have fallen from Takeo's horse, Raku, the little gray horse he had given her; yes, she had fallen, and she had lost his child.

Her eyes filled with tears. She knew she was not thinking clearly, but she knew the child was gone. She felt Shizuka's hand move and then it returned holding a cloth, slightly warmed, to wipe her face.

"Lady!" Shizuka said. "Lady Kaede."

Kaede tried to move her own hand, but it seemed to be immobilized, and something pricked her there too.

"Don't try to move," Shizuka said. "Lord Fujiwara's physician, Dr. Ishida, has been treating you. You are going to get well now. Don't cry, lady!"

"It's normal," she heard the physician say. "Those who come close to death always weep when they are brought back, whether from joy or sorrow I've never been able to tell."

Kaede herself did not know. The tears flowed, and when they finally stopped, she fell asleep.

For several days she slept, woke, ate a little, and slept again. Then she slept less but lay with her eyes closed, listening to the household around her. She heard Hana's voice regaining its confidence, Ai's gentle tone, Shizuka singing and scolding Hana, who had taken to following her around like a shadow, trying to please her. It was a house of women—the men stayed away—women who were aware they had come close to the brink of disaster, were still not out of danger, but so far had survived. Autumn slowly turned to winter.

The only man was the physician, who stayed in the guest pavilion and visited her every day. He was small and deft, with long-fingered hands and a quiet voice. Kaede came to trust him, sensing that he did not judge her. He did not think her good or bad—indeed, he did not think in such terms at all. He only wanted to see her recover.

He used techniques he had learned on the mainland: needles of gold and silver, a paste of mugwort leaves burned on the skin, and teas brewed from willow bark. He was the first person she had ever met who had traveled there.

Sometimes she lay and listened to his voice telling Hana stories of the animals he had seen, huge whales in the sea and bears and tigers on land.

When she was able to get up and walk outside, it was Dr. Ishida who suggested that a ceremony should be held for the lost child. Kaede was carried to the temple in a palanquin, and she knelt for a long time before the shrine to Jizo, the one who looks after the water children who die before they are born. She grieved for the child whose moment of life had been so brief, conceived and extinguished in the midst of violence. Yet, it had been a child begun in love.

I will never forget you, she promised in her heart, and prayed it would have a safer passage next time. She felt its spirit was now safe until it began the journey of life again. She made the same prayer for Shigeru's child, realizing she was the only person apart from Shizuka who knew of its brief moment of existence. The tears flowed again, but when she returned home she did indeed feel that a weight had been lifted from her.

"Now you must take up life again," Dr. Ishida told her. "You are young: You will marry and have other children."

"I think I am destined not to marry," Kaede replied.

He smiled, assuming she was joking. Of course, she

thought, it was a joke. Women in her position, of her rank, always married, or rather *were married* to whoever seemed to offer the most advantageous alliance. But such marriages were arranged by fathers, or clan leaders, or other overlords, and she seemed suddenly to be free of all these. Her father was dead, as were most of his senior retainers. The Seishuu clan, to which both the Maruyama and Shirakawa families belonged, was fully occupied with the turmoil that had followed the downfall of the Tohan and the sudden unexpected rise of Arai Daiichi. Who was there to tell her what to do? Was it Arai now? Should she be making a formal alliance with him, recognizing him as her overlord? And what were the advantages or disadvantages of such a move?

"You have grown very serious," he said. "May I ask what is occupying your mind? You must try not to worry."

"I have to decide what to do," she said.

"I suggest doing nothing until you are stronger. Winter is nearly upon us. You must rest, eat well, and be very careful not to take a chill."

And I must consolidate my lands, contact Sugita Hiroki at Maruyama, and tell him I mean to take up my inheritance, and find money and food for my men, she thought, but did not speak this aloud to Ishida.

As she grew stronger she began to restore the house before the snows began. Everything was washed, new matting laid, screens repaired, tiles and shingles replaced. The garden was tended again. She had little money to pay for anything, but she found men to work for her on the promise of payment in the spring, and every day she learned more of how a look or a tone of voice won her their devoted service.

She moved into her father's rooms, where at last she had unrestricted access to his books. She read and practiced writing for hours at a time, until Shizuka, fearing for her health, brought Hana to distract her. Then Kaede played with her sister, teaching her to read and use the brush like a man. Under Shizuka's strict care Hana had lost some of her wildness. She was as hungry for learning as Kaede.

"We should both have been born boys," Kaede sighed.

"Father would have been proud of us, then," Hana said. Her tongue was pressed against her upper teeth as she concentrated on the characters.

Kaede did not reply. She never spoke of her father and tried not to think about him. Indeed, she could no longer clearly distinguish between what had actually happened when he died and the feverish imaginings of her illness. She did not question Shizuka and Kondo, afraid of their replies. She had been to the temple, performed the rites of mourning, and ordered a fine stone to be carved for his grave, but she still feared his ghost, which had hovered at the edge of the redness of her fever. Though she clung to the thought *I have done nothing wrong,* she could not remember him without a twinge of shame, which she masked with anger.

He will be more helpful to me dead than alive, she decided, and let it be known that she was reverting to the name of Shirakawa, since it had been her father's will that she should be his heir and should remain in the family home. When Shoji returned to the house after the period of mourning and began to go through the records and accounts with her, she thought she detected some disapproval in his attitude, but the accounts were in such a terrible state that she used her anger to cow him. It was hard to believe affairs had been allowed to deteriorate so badly. It seemed impossible to secure enough food for the men she had already and their families, let alone any others she might hope to employ. It was her main source of anxiety.

With Kondo she went though the armor and weapons and gave instructions for repairs to be done and replacements ordered. She came to rely more and more on his experience and judgment. He suggested she should reestablish the domain's borders, to prevent encroachment and to maintain the warriors' fighting skills. She agreed, knowing instinctively she had to keep the men occupied and interested. For the first time she found herself grateful for the years in the castle, for she realized how much she had learned about warriors and weapons. From then on, Kondo often rode out with five or six men, making use of these expeditions to bring back information, too.

She told Kondo and Shizuka to let pieces of information fall among the men: an alliance with Arai, the campaign for Maruyama in the spring, the possibility of advancement and wealth.

She saw nothing of Lord Fujiwara, though he sent gifts: quail, dried persimmons, wine, and warm quilted clothes. Ishida returned to the nobleman's residence, and she knew the doctor would inform him of her progress, and certainly would not dare keep any secrets from him. She did not want to meet Fujiwara. It was shameful to have deceived him, and she regretted the loss of his regard for her, but she was also relieved not to see him face-to-face. His intense interest in her unnerved and repelled her, as much as his white skin and cormorant eyes.

"He is a useful ally," Shizuka told her. They were in the garden, overseeing the replacement of the crushed stone lantern. It was a cool clear day, of rare sunshine.

Kaede was watching a pair of ibis in the rice fields beyond the gate. Their pale pink winter plumage glowed against the bare earth.

"He's been very kind to me," she said. "I know I owe my life to him, through Dr. Ishida. But it would not trouble me if I never saw him again."

The ibis followed each other through the pools that had collected in the corner of the fields, their curved bills stirring up the muddy water.

"Anyway," she added, "I am flawed for him now. He will despise me more than ever."

Shizuka had said nothing of the nobleman's desire to marry Kaede, and she did not mention it now.

"You must make some decisions," she said quietly. "Otherwise we will all starve before spring."

"I am reluctant to approach anyone," Kaede said. "I must not seem like a supplicant, desperate and needy. I know I must go to Arai eventually, but I think it can wait till winter is over."

"I believe the birds will begin to gather before then," Shizuka said. "Arai will send someone to you, I expect."

"And what about you, Shizuka?" Kaede said. The pillar was in position and the new lantern in place. Tonight she would place a lamp in it; it would look beautiful in the frosty garden under the clear sky. "What will you do? I don't suppose you will stay with me forever, will you? You must have other concerns. What about your sons? You must long to see them. And what are your commands from the Tribe?"

"Nothing more at the moment than to continue looking after your interests," Shizuka replied.

"Would they have taken the child as they took Takeo?" Kaede said, and then immediately added, "Oh, don't answer me, there is no point now." She felt the tears threaten and pressed her lips firmly together. She was silent for a few moments and then went on, "I suppose you keep them informed of my actions and decisions too?"

"I send messages from time to time to my uncle—when I thought you were close to death, for instance. And I would tell him of any new developments: if you were to decide to marry again, that sort of thing."

"I won't be doing that." As the afternoon light began to fade, the pink plumage of the ibis glowed more deeply. It was very still. Now that the workmen had finished, the garden seemed more silent than ever. And in the silence she heard again the promise of the White Goddess: *Be patient.*

I will marry no one but him, she vowed again. *I will be patient.*

It was the last day of sunshine. The weather became damp and raw. A few days later Kondo returned from one of his patrols in a rainstorm. Dismounting rapidly, he called to the women in the house, "There are strangers on the road: Lord Arai's men, five or six, and horses."

Kaede told him to assemble as many men as possible and give the impression there were many more at call.

"Tell the women to prepare food," she said to Shizuka. "Everything we have, make it lavish. We must seem to be prospering. Help me change my clothes, and bring my sisters. Then you must stay out of sight."

She put on the most elegant robe that Fujiwara had given her, remembering as she always did the day she had promised it to Hana.

She will get it when it fits her, she thought, *and I swear I will be there to see her wear it.*

Hana and Ai entered the room, Hana chattering excitedly and jumping up and down to keep warm. Ayame followed, carrying a brazier. Kaede winced when she saw how full of charcoal it was: They would shiver more when Arai's men were gone.

"Who is coming?" Ai asked nervously. Ever since their father's death and Kaede's illness she had become more fragile, as if the combined shocks had weakened her.

"Arai's men. We have to make a good impression. That's why I've borrowed Hana's robe back again."

"Don't get it dirty, Older Sister," Hana said, groaning as Ayame began to comb out her hair. Usually she wore it tied back. Loose, it was longer than she was tall.

"What do they want?" Ai had gone pale.

"I expect they will tell us," Kaede replied.

"Do I have to be here?" Ai pleaded.

"Yes. Put on the other robe Lord Fujiwara sent, and help Hana dress. We must all be here together when they arrive."

"Why?" Hana said.

Kaede did not answer. She herself hardly knew the

reason. She had had a sudden image of the three of them in the lonely house, the three daughters of Lord Shirakawa, remote, beautiful, dangerous. . . . That was how they must appear to Arai's warriors.

"All-merciful, all-compassionate one, help me," she prayed to the White Goddess as Shizuka tied her sash and combed out her hair.

She heard the tread of the horses' feet outside the gate, heard Kondo call a welcome to the men. His voice hit just the right note of courtesy and confidence, and she thanked heaven for the Tribe's acting skills and hoped hers would be as great.

"Ayame, show our visitors to the guest pavilion," she said. "Give them tea and food. The best tea and the finest pottery. When they've finished eating, ask their leader to come here to speak with me. Hana, if you are ready, come and sit down next to me."

Shizuka helped Ai with her robe and quickly combed her hair. "I will hide where I can hear," she whispered.

"Open the shutters before you go," Kaede said. "We will get the last of the sun." For the rain had ceased and a fitful sun cast a silvery light over the garden and into the room.

"What do I have to do?" Hana said, kneeling beside Kaede.

"When the men come in, you must bow at exactly the same moment I do. And then just look as beautiful as you can and sit without moving a muscle while I talk."

"Is that all?" Hana was disappointed.

"Watch the men; study them without seeming to. You can tell me afterward what you thought of them. You, too, Ai. You must give nothing away, react to nothing—like statues."

Ai came and knelt on Kaede's other side. She was trembling but was able to compose herself.

The sun's last rays streamed into the room, setting the dust motes dancing and lighting up the three girls. The newly cleared waterfall, made louder by the rain, could be heard from the garden. A shadow flashed blue as a kingfisher dove from a rock.

From the guest room came the murmur of the men's voices. Kaede imagined she could catch their unfamiliar smell. It made her tense. She straightened her back and her mind turned to ice. She would meet their power with her own. She would remember how easily they could die.

In a little while she heard Ayame's voice telling the men Lady Shirakawa would receive them now. Shortly after, their leader and one of his companions approached the main house and stepped onto the veranda. Ayame dropped to her knees at the edge of the room, and the retainer also knelt outside. As the other man crossed the threshold Kaede let him see the three of them and then bowed to him, touching her forehead to the floor. Hana and Ai moved at exactly the same time.

The three girls sat up in unison.

The warrior knelt and announced, "I am Akita Tsutomu from Inuyama. I have been sent to Lady Shirakawa by Lord Arai."

He bowed and stayed low. Kaede said, "Welcome, Lord Akita. I am grateful to you for your arduous journey and to Lord Arai for sending you. I am eager to learn how I may serve him." She added, "You may sit up."

He did so, and she gazed frankly at him. She knew women were supposed to keep their eyes cast down in the presence of men, but she hardly felt like a woman anymore. She wondered if she would ever be that sort of woman again. She realized Hana and Ai were staring in the same way at Akita, with opaque, unreadable eyes.

He was approaching middle age, his hair still black but beginning to thin. His nose was small but slightly hooked, like a bird's, giving him a rapacious look, offset by a well-formed mouth with rather large lips. His clothes were travel-stained but of good quality. His hands were square and short-fingered, with strong, splayed thumbs. She guessed he was a practical man, but also a conspirator, given to trickery. There was nothing there to trust.

"Lord Arai asks after your health," he said, looking at each of the sisters, then returning his gaze to Kaede. "It was reported that you were unwell."

"I am recovered," she replied. "You may thank Lord Arai for his concern."

He inclined his head slightly. He seemed ill at ease, as if he were more at home among men than among women and unsure of how to address her. She wondered how much he had heard of her situation, if he knew the cause of her illness.

"We heard with great regret of Lord Shirakawa's death," he went on. "Lord Arai has been concerned about your lack of protection and wishes to make it clear that he considers you to be in as strong an alliance with him as if you were part of his family."

Hana and Ai turned their heads, exchanged a look with each other, then resumed their silent staring. It seemed to unnerve Akita even more. He cleared his throat. "That being the case, Lord Arai wishes to receive you and your sisters at Inuyama to discuss the alliance and Lady Shirakawa's future."

Impossible, she thought, though she said nothing for a few moments. Then she spoke, smiling slightly: "Nothing would give me greater pleasure. However, my health is not strong enough to permit me to travel yet, and as we are still mourning our father, it is not fitting that we should leave home. It is late in the year. We will arrange a visit to Inuyama in the spring. You may tell Lord Arai that I consider our alliance unbroken and I am grateful to him for his protection. I will consult him as far as I am able and keep him informed of my decisions."

Again the look between Hana and Ai flashed through the room like lightning. *It really is uncanny,* Kaede thought, and suddenly wanted to laugh.

Akita said, "I must urge Lady Shirakawa to return with me."

"It is quite impossible," she said, meeting his gaze and

adding, "It is not for you to urge me to do anything."

The rebuke surprised him. A flush of color spread around his neck and up to his cheekbones.

Hana and Ai leaned forward very slightly and their gaze intensified. The sun went behind clouds, darkening the room, and there was a sudden rush of rain on the roof. The bamboo wind chimes rang with a hollow note.

Akita said, "I apologize. Of course you must do as seems fitting to you."

"I will come to Inuyama in the spring," she repeated. "You may tell Lord Arai that. You are welcome to spend the night here, but I think you will need to leave in the morning to get back before the snow."

"Lady Shirakawa." He bowed to the floor. As he shuffled out backward she asked, "Who are your companions?" She spoke abruptly, allowing impatience to creep into her voice, knowing instinctively that she had dominated him. Something about the scene, her sisters, her own demeanor, had cowed him. She could almost smell it.

"My sister's son, Sonoda Mitsuru, and three of my own retainers."

"Leave your nephew here. He may enter my service for

the winter and escort us to Inuyama. He will be a guarantee of your good faith."

He stared at the ground, taken aback at the request; yet, she thought with anger, any man in her position would have demanded the same. With the young man in her household, his uncle would be less likely to misrepresent her or otherwise betray her to Arai.

"Of course, trust between us is a symbol of my trust in Lord Arai," Kaede said, more impatiently, as he hesitated.

"I see no reason why he should not stay here," Akita conceded.

I have a hostage, she thought, and marveled at the sense of power it gave her.

She bowed to Akita, Hana and Ai copying her, while he prostrated himself before them. Rain was still falling when he left, but the sun had struggled out again, turning to fragmented rainbows the drops of water that clung to the bare branches and the last of the autumn leaves. She made a sign to her sisters not to move.

Before Akita entered the guest room, he turned to look back at them. They sat motionless until he was out of sight. The sun vanished and the rain streamed down.

Ayame stood from where she had been kneeling in the shadows and closed the shutters. Kaede turned and hugged Hana.

"Did I do well?" Hana asked, her eyes lengthened and full of emotion.

"It was brilliant, almost like magic. But what was that look between you?"

"We should not have done it," Ai said, ashamed. "It's so childish. We used to do it when Mother or Ayame was teaching us. Hana started it. They never knew if they were imagining it or not. We never dared do it in front of Father. And to do it to a great lord . . ."

"It just seemed to happen," Hana said, laughing. "He didn't like it, did he? His eyes went all jumpy and he started to sweat."

"He is hardly a great lord," Kaede said. "Arai might have sent someone of higher rank."

"Would you have done what he asked, then? Would we have gone back with him to Inuyama?"

"Even if Arai himself had come, I would not," Kaede replied. "I will always make them wait for me."

"Do you want to know what else I noticed?" Hana said.

"Tell me."

"Lord Akita was afraid of you, Older Sister."

"You have sharp eyes," Kaede said, laughing.

"I don't want to go away," Ai said. "I never want to leave home."

Kaede gazed at her sister with pity. "You will have to marry someday. You may have to go to Inuyama next year and stay for a while."

"Will I have to?" Hana asked.

"Maybe," Kaede said. "Lots of men will want to marry you."

For the sake of an alliance with me, she thought, saddened that she would have to use her sisters so.

"I'll only go if Shizuka comes with us," Hana declared.

Kaede smiled and hugged her again. There was no point in telling her that Shizuka could never go in safety to Inuyama while Arai was there. "Go and tell Shizuka to come to me. Ayame, you had better see what meal we can give these men tonight."

"I'm glad you told them to leave tomorrow," Ayame said. "I don't think we could afford to feed them for longer. They are too used to eating well." She shook her head. "Though

I have to say, Lady Kaede, I don't think your father would have approved of your conduct."

"You don't have to say it," Kaede retorted swiftly. "And if you want to stay in this household, you will never speak to me like that again."

Ayame flinched at her tone. "Lady Shirakawa," she said dully, dropped to her knees, and crawled backward from the room.

Shizuka came in shortly, carrying a lamp, for dusk was now falling. Kaede told her sisters to go and change their clothes.

"How much did you hear?" she demanded when they had gone.

"Enough, and Kondo told me what Lord Akita said when he went back to the pavilion. He thought there was some supernatural power at work in this house. You terrified him. He said you were like the autumn spider, golden and deadly, weaving a web of beauty to captivate men."

"Quite poetic," Kaede remarked.

"Yes, Kondo thought so too!"

Kaede could picture the ironic gleam in his eyes. One day, she promised herself, he would look at her without irony.

He would take her seriously. They all would, all these men who thought they were so powerful.

"And my hostage, Sonoda Mitsuru, is he terrified too?"

"Your hostage!" Shizuka laughed. "How did you dare suggest that?"

"Was I wrong?"

"No, on the contrary, it made them believe you are much stronger than was first thought. The young man is a little apprehensive about being left here. Where do you intend to put him?"

"Shoji can take him in his house and look after him. I certainly don't want him here." Kaede paused, then went on with a trace of bitterness, "He will be better treated than I was. But what about you? He will not be any danger to you, will he?"

"Arai must know I am still with you," Shizuka said. "I see no danger from this young man. His uncle, Lord Akita, will be careful not to upset you now. Your strength protects me—all of us. Arai probably expected to find you distraught and desperate for his help. He will hear a very different story. I told you the birds would gather."

"So, who do we expect next?"

"I believe someone will come from Maruyama before the onset of winter, in response to the messengers Kondo sent."

Kaede was hoping for the same thing, her mind often turning to her last meeting with her kinswoman and the promise that had been made then. Her father had told her she would have to fight for that inheritance, but she hardly knew who her adversaries would be or how to set about going to war. Who would teach her how to do it; who would lead an army on her behalf?

She said farewell the next day to Akita and his men, thankful that their stay was so short, and welcomed his nephew, summoning Shoji and handing him over. She was aware of her effect on the young man—he could not take his eyes off her and trembled in her presence—but he did not interest her at all, other than as her hostage.

"Keep him busy," she told Shoji. "Treat him well and with respect, but don't let him know too much of our affairs."

Over the next few weeks men began to turn up at her gate. Some secret message had gone out that she was taking on warriors. They came singly or in twos and threes, never in large groups, men whose masters were dead or dispossessed, the straggling remnants of years of war. She and Kondo devised tests for them—she did not want rogues or fools—but they did not turn many away, for most were experienced fighters who would form the kernel of her army when spring came. Nevertheless, Kaede despaired of being able to feed and keep them all through the long winter.

A few days before the solstice, Kondo came to her with the news she had been waiting for.

"Lord Sugita from Maruyama is here with several of his men."

She welcomed them with delight. They revered the memory of Lady Maruyama and were accustomed to seeing a woman as a leader. She was especially glad to see Sugita, remembering him from the journey to Tsuwano. He had left them there to return home, to ensure the domain was not attacked and taken over during Lady Maruyama's absence. Filled with grief at her death, he was determined her wishes should be fulfilled. A man of great practicality, he had also brought rice and other provisions with him.

"I will not add to your burdens," he told Kaede.

"They are not so heavy that we cannot feed old friends," she lied.

"Everyone is going to suffer this winter," he replied gloomily. "The storms, Iida's death, Arai's campaigns—the harvest is a fraction of what it should be."

Kaede invited him to eat with her, something she did with none of the others, whom she left to Shoji and Kondo to look after. They talked briefly about the events at Inuyama, and then at length about the Maruyama inheritance. He treated Kaede with respect, colored by an affectionate familiarity, as if he were an uncle or a cousin. She felt at ease with him: He was not threatened by her but he took her seriously.

When they had finished eating and the dishes had been cleared away he said, "It was my lady's desire to see her domain in your care. I was delighted to receive your message that you intend to take up your inheritance. I came at once to tell you that I will help you; many of us will. We should start to plan our actions before spring."

"It is my intention, and I'll need all the help I can get," Kaede replied. "I have no idea how to set about it. Will I be able simply to take the lands over? Who do they belong to now?"

"They belong to you," he said. "You are the next female heir, and it was our lady's express wish that the domain be yours. But several other people lay claim to it: The main contender is Lady Maruyama's stepdaughter, who is married to a cousin of Lord Iida. Arai has not been able to eradicate him, and he has quite a large force: a mixture of Tohan who fled from Noguchi Castle when it fell, and disaffected Seishuu who see no reason why they should submit to Arai. They are wintering in the far west, but they will march on Maruyama in the spring. If you do not move swiftly and boldly, the domain will be fought over and destroyed."

"I promised Lady Naomi that I would prevent that from happening," Kaede said, "but I didn't know what I was promising or how to achieve it."

"There are many people willing to help you," he said, leaning forward and whispering: "I was sent by our council of elders to request that you come to us, and soon. The domain prospered under Lady Naomi; we all had enough to eat, and even the poorest could feed their children. We traded with the mainland, mined silver and copper, established many small industries. The alliance between Lord Arai, Lord Otori Shigeru, and the Maruyama would have extended that prosperity all the way into the Middle Country. We want to save what we can of the alliance."

"I plan to visit Lord Arai in the spring," Kaede said. "I will formalize our alliance then."

"Then one of your terms must be that he supports you in your claim to Maruyama. Only Arai is strong enough to dissuade the stepdaughter and her husband to retire without fighting. And if it comes to battle, only his army will be large enough to beat them. You must move quickly; as soon as the roads are open again you must go to Inuyama and then come to us, with Arai's backing."

He looked at her, smiled slightly, and said, "I am sorry, I do not mean to seem to be commanding you in any way. But I hope you will take my advice."

"I will," she said. "It is what I had already thought of doing, but with your support I am encouraged in it."

They went on to talk of how many men Sugita could raise, and he swore he would hand over the domain to no one but her. He said he would leave the next day, as he wanted to be back at Maruyama before the new year. Then he said casually, "It's a shame Otori Takeo is dead. If you had married him, his name and the Otori connection would have made you even stronger."

Kaede's heart seemed to stop beating and fall from her

chest to her stomach. "I had not heard of his death," she said, trying to keep her voice steady.

"Well, it's only what people are saying. I don't know any details. I suppose it's the obvious explanation for his disappearance. It may be only a rumor."

"Maybe," Kaede said, while thinking silently, *Or maybe he is dead in an open field or on the mountain and I will never know.* "I am growing tired, Lord Sugita. Forgive me."

"Lady Shirakawa." He bowed to her and stood. "We'll keep in touch as much as the weather allows. I will expect you at Maruyama in the spring; the clan's forces will support your claim. If anything changes, I will get word to you somehow."

She promised to do the same, impatient for him to be gone. When he had left and she was sure he was safely inside the guest pavilion, she called for Shizuka, paced up and down, and when the girl came she seized her with both hands.

"Are you keeping something from me?"

"Lady?" Shizuka looked at her in surprise. "What do you mean? What's happened?"

"Sugita said he'd heard Takeo was dead."

"It's just a rumor."

"But you've heard it?"

"Yes. I don't believe it, though. If he were dead, we would have been told. You look so pale! Sit down. You must not overtire yourself; you must not get sick again. I'll prepare the beds."

She led her from the main room into the room where they slept. Kaede sank to the floor, her heart still thudding. "I am so afraid he will die before I see him again."

Shizuka knelt beside her, untied her sash, and helped her out of the formal robes she had been wearing.

"I'll massage your head. Sit still."

Kaede was restlessly moving her head from side to side, clutching her hair, clenching and unclenching her fists. Shizuka's hands in her hair did not soothe her; they simply reminded her of the unbearable afternoon at Inuyama and the events that followed. She was shivering.

"You must find out, Shizuka; I must know for sure. Send a message to your uncle. Send Kondo. He must leave at once."

"I thought you were beginning to forget him," Shizuka murmured, her hands working at Kaede's scalp.

"I cannot forget him. I've tried, but as soon as I hear his name, it all returns to me. Do you remember the day I first saw him at Tsuwano? I fell in love with him at that moment. A fever came over me. It was—it is—an enchantment, a sickness from which I can never be cured. You said we would get over it, but we never will."

Her brow was burning beneath Shizuka's fingers. Alarmed, the girl asked, "Shall I send for Ishida?"

"I am tormented by desire," Kaede said in a low voice. "Dr. Ishida can do nothing for that."

"Desire is simple enough to alleviate," Shizuka replied calmly.

"But my desire is only for him. Nothing—no one else—can relieve it. I know I must try to live without him. I have duties to my family that I must—I will—carry out. But if he is dead, you must tell me."

"I will write to Kenji," Shizuka promised. "I'll send Kondo tomorrow, though we cannot really spare him. . . ."

"Send him," Kaede said.

Shizuka made an infusion from the willow twigs that Ishida had left, and persuaded Kaede to drink it, but her sleep was restless and in the morning she was listless and feverish.

Ishida came, applied mugwort and used his needles,

rebuking her gently for not taking better care of herself.

"It's not serious," he told Shizuka when they stepped outside. "It will pass in a day or two. She is too sensitive and makes too many demands on herself. She should marry."

"She will only agree to marry one man—and that is impossible," Shizuka said.

"The father of the child?"

Shizuka nodded. "Yesterday she heard a rumor that he was dead. The fever started then."

"Ah." His eyes had a thoughtful, faraway look. She wondered what or whom he was remembering from his youth.

"I fear the coming months," she said. "Once we are closed in by snow, I am afraid she will begin to brood."

"I have a letter for her from Lord Fujiwara. He would like her to visit him and stay for a few days. The change of scene may help to lift her spirits and distract her."

"Lord Fujiwara is too kind to this house and pays us too great an attention." Shizuka used the formal words of thanks automatically as she took the letter. She was acutely aware of the man next to her, of their hands touching briefly. The distant look in his eyes had sparked something in her. During Kaede's illness they had spent many hours together, and she had come to admire his patience and skill. He was kind, unlike most men she had known.

"Will you come again tomorrow?" she said, glancing at him.

"Of course. You can give me Lady Kaede's reply to the letter. You will accompany her to Lord Fujiwara's?"

"Of course!" She repeated his words playfully. He smiled and touched her again, deliberately, on the arm. The pressure of his fingers made her shiver. It was so long since she had slept with a man. She had a sudden strong desire to feel his hands all over her body; she wanted to lie down with him and hold him. He deserved it for his kindness.

"Till tomorrow," he said, his eyes warm, as if he had recognized her feelings and shared them.

She slipped into her sandals and ran to call the servants with the palanquin.

Kaede's fever subsided, and by evening she had recovered some of her energy. She had lain still all day, warm under a huge pile of quilts, next to the brazier that Ayame had insisted on lighting, thinking about the future. Takeo might be dead;

the child certainly was. Her heart wanted only to follow them to the next world, but her reason told her it would be sheer weakness to throw her life away and abandon those who depended on her. A woman might act like that; a man in her position never would.

Shizuka is right, she thought, *there is only one person I know who can help me now. I must see what arrangement I can come to with Fujiwara.*

Shizuka gave her the letter that Ishida had brought that morning. Fujiwara had also sent gifts for the new year, specially shaped rice cakes, dried sardines and sweetened chestnuts, rolled kelp and rice wine. Hana and Ai were busy in the kitchen, helping to prepare for the festival.

"He flatters me; he writes in men's language saying he knows I understand it," Kaede said. "But there are so many characters I don't know." She sighed deeply. "There's so much I need to learn. Is one winter going to be enough?"

"Will you go to Lord Fujiwara's?"

"I suppose so. He might teach me. Do you think he would?"

"There's nothing he'd like more," Shizuka said dryly.

"I thought he would want nothing more to do with me,

185

but he says he has been waiting for my recovery. I am better—as well as I will ever be." Kaede's voice was doubtful. "I must be better. I have to look after my sisters, my land, my men."

"As I've said many times, Fujiwara is your best ally in this."

"Maybe not the best: the only. But I don't really trust him. What does he want from me?"

"What do *you* want from *him*?" Shizuka replied.

"That's simple: on the one hand, learning; on the other, money and food to raise an army and feed it. But what do I offer him in return?"

Shizuka wondered if she should mention Fujiwara's desire for marriage, but decided against it, fearing it would disturb Kaede to the point of fever again. Let the nobleman speak for himself. She was sure he would.

"He addresses me as Lady Shirakawa. I am ashamed to face him, after deceiving him."

"He will have learned of your father's wishes regarding your name," Shizuka said. "Everyone knows that your father named you as his heir before his death. We have made sure of that."

Kaede glanced at her to see if she was mocking her, but

Shizuka's face was serious. "Of course, I had to do as my father requested," Kaede agreed.

"There is nothing else Lord Fujiwara needs to know, then. Filial obedience comes before everything."

"So K'ung Fu-Tzu tells me," Kaede said. "Lord Fujiwara *needs* to know nothing else but I suspect he *wants* to know a great deal more. If he is still interested in me, that is."

"He will be," Shizuka assured her, thinking that Kaede was more beautiful than ever. Her illness and grief had removed the last traces of childishness from her and had given her expression depth and mystery.

They celebrated the new year with Fujiwara's gifts, and ate buckwheat noodles, and black beans that Ayame had put away at the end of the summer. At midnight they went to the temple and listened to the priests' chanting and the bells' tolling for the extinction of human passions. Kaede knew she should pray to be freed from them all and to be purified, but found herself asking for what she most desired—for Takeo to be alive—and then for money and power.

The following day the women of the household took candles, incense, and lanterns, wrinkled mandarins, sweet chestnuts, and dried persimmons, and went to the caves where the Shirakawa river emerged from a series of underground caverns. Here they performed their own ceremonies before the rock that the water had turned into the shape of the White Goddess. No men were ever supposed to come into this place; if they did, the mountain might fall and the Shirakawa might be extinguished. An aged couple lived behind the shrine at the entrance to the cave; only the old woman went inside to take offerings to the goddess. Kaede knelt on the damp rock, listening to the ancient voice mumble words she hardly knew the meaning of. She thought of her mother and Lady Maruyama and asked for their help and their intercession. She realized how much this holy place meant to her, and she felt that the goddess was watching over her.

The next day she went to Lord Fujiwara's. Hana was bitterly disappointed at being left behind, and wept when she had to say good-bye not only to Kaede but also to Shizuka.

"It's only for a few days," Kaede said.

"Why can't I come with you?"

"Lord Fujiwara did not invite you. Besides, you would hate it there. You would have to behave properly, speak in formal language, and sit still most of the day."

"Will you hate it?"

"I expect I will," Kaede sighed.

"At least you will eat delicious food," Hana said, adding longingly, "Quail!"

"If we are eating his food, there will be more for you here," Kaede replied. It was in fact one of the reasons she was happy to be away for a while, for no matter how many times she looked at the food stores and calculated the days of winter, it remained obvious that they would run out of food before spring.

"And someone has to entertain young Mitsuru," Shizuka added. "You must make sure he is not too homesick."

"Ai can do that," Hana retorted. "He likes Ai."

Kaede had noticed the same thing. Her sister had not admitted any affection in return, but she was shy about such matters—and anyway, Kaede thought, what difference did her feelings make? Ai would have to be betrothed soon. The new year had seen her turn fourteen. It might be that Sonoda Mitsuru, if his uncle were to adopt him, would be a good match, but she would not relinquish her sister cheaply.

In a year they will be lining up for marriages with the Shirakawa, she told herself.

Ai had colored a little at Hana's remark. "Take care of

yourself, Older Sister," she said, embracing Kaede. "Don't worry about us. I'll look after everything here."

"We are not far away," Kaede replied. "You must send for me if you think I am needed." She could not help adding, "And if any messages come for me—if Kondo returns—let me know at once."

They arrived at Lord Fujiwara's in the early afternoon. The day had begun mild and overcast, but even as they traveled the wind swung to the northeast and the temperature dropped.

Mamoru met them, conveyed the nobleman's greetings, and led them, not to the guest rooms where they had stayed before, but to another, smaller pavilion, less ornately decorated but to Kaede's eyes even more beautiful with its elegant simplicity and muted colors. She was grateful for this thoughtfulness, for she had been dreading seeing her father's angry ghost in the room where her secret had been revealed to him.

"Lord Fujiwara thought Lady Shirakawa would prefer to rest this evening," Mamoru said quietly. "He will receive you tomorrow, if that is agreeable to you."

"Thank you," Kaede said. "Please tell Lord Fujiwara I am completely at his service. I will do whatever he desires."

She was already aware of tension. Mamoru had used her name without hesitation—had glanced at her swiftly when she arrived, as if trying to discern any change in her, but since then had not looked at her at all. However, she knew already how much he saw of her without appearing to. She straightened her back and gazed at him with a hint of disdain in her expression. Let him study her all he liked as a subject for the roles he played onstage. He would never be other than a counterfeit of what she was. She did not care what he thought of her. But she did care what Fujiwara thought. *He must despise me,* she told herself, *but if he shows it by so much as a flicker of one eyebrow, I'll leave and never see him again, no matter what he might do for me.*

She was relieved that the meeting was to be postponed. Ishida paid them a call and checked her pulse and eyes. He told her he would prepare a new sort of tea that would purify the blood and strengthen the stomach, and asked her to send Shizuka to his rooms the following day to collect it.

A hot bath had been prepared, making Kaede warm not only from the water but also with envy at the amount of wood available to heat it. Afterward food was brought to their room by maids who hardly spoke at all.

"It is the traditional ladies' winter meal," Shizuka exclaimed when she saw the delicacies of the season, raw sea bream and squid, broiled eel with green perilla and horseradish, pickled cucumbers and salted lotus root, rare black mushrooms and burdock, laid out on the lacquer trays. "This is what they would eat in the capital. I wonder how many other women in the Three Countries are eating something this exquisite tonight!"

"Everything is exquisite here," Kaede replied. *How easy it is*, she thought, *to have luxury and taste when you have money!*

They had finished eating and were thinking about retiring, when there was a tap outside the door.

"The maids have come to prepare the beds," Shizuka said, and went to the door. But when she slid it open, it was Mamoru who stood outside. There was snow on his hair.

"Forgive me," he said, "but the first snow of the year has begun to fall. Lord Fujiwara wishes to visit Lady Shirakawa. The view from this pavilion is particularly fine."

"This is Lord Fujiwara's house," Kaede said. "I am his guest. Whatever is his pleasure is mine also."

Mamoru left and she heard him speak to the maids. A few moments later two of them came to the room with warm red quilted robes, which they dressed her in. Accompanied by Shizuka, she went out onto the veranda. Animal skins had been placed over cushions for them to sit on. Lanterns had been hung from the trees, lighting the falling flakes. The ground was already white. A garden of rocks lay under two pine trees that grew in low, beautifully trained patterns, framing the view. Behind them the dull mass of the mountain was just visible through the swirling snow. Kaede was silent, transfixed by the beauty of the scene, its silent purity.

Moving so quietly that they hardly heard him, Lord Fujiwara approached them. They both knelt before him.

"Lady Shirakawa," he said. "I am so grateful to you, first for condescending to visit my humble place, and second for indulging my whim to share the first snow viewing with you.

"Please sit up," he added. "You must wrap yourself up well; you must not catch cold."

Servants filed behind him bringing braziers, flasks of wine, cups, and furs. Mamoru took one of the furs and placed it over her shoulders, then wrapped another around Fujiwara as he sat beside her. Kaede stroked the pelt with a mixture of delight and revulsion.

"They come from the mainland," Fujiwara told her after

they had exchanged formal greetings. "Ishida brings them back when he goes on his expeditions there."

"What animal is it?"

"Some kind of bear, I believe."

She could not imagine a bear so large. She tried to picture it in its native land, so distant and foreign to her. It would be powerful, slow-moving, ferocious, yet men had killed and skinned it. She wondered if its spirit still dwelt somehow in the skin and if it would resent her wearing its warmth. She shivered. "Dr. Ishida is brave as well as clever, to go on such dangerous journeys."

"He has an unquenchable thirst for knowledge, it seems. Of course, it has all been rewarded by Lady Shirakawa's recovery."

"I owe him my life," she said in a low voice.

"Then he is even more precious to me than on his own account."

She detected his usual irony, but no contempt. Indeed, he could hardly be more flattering.

"How lovely the first snow is," she said. "Yet, by the end of winter we long for it to melt."

"Snow pleases me," he said. "I like its whiteness and the

way it wraps the world. Beneath it everything becomes clean."

Mamoru poured wine and passed it to them. Then he vanished into the shadows. The servants withdrew. They were not really alone, but there was an illusion of solitude, as though nothing existed but the two of them, the glowing braziers, the heavy animal furs, and the snow.

After they had watched it in silence for a while, Fujiwara called to the servants to bring more lamps.

"I want to see your face," he said, leaning forward and studying her in the same hungry way he had gazed on his treasures. Kaede raised her eyes and looked past him at the snow, now falling more thickly, swirling in the light from the lanterns, blocking out the mountains, blurring the outside world.

"Possibly more beautiful than ever," he said quietly. She thought she detected a note of relief in his voice. She knew that if her illness had marred her in any way, he would have withdrawn politely and would never have seen her again. They could all have starved to death at Shirakawa with no gesture of compassion or help from him. *How cold he is,* she thought, and felt her own body chill in response; yet, she made no sign of it, just continued to gaze past him, letting the snow fill her eyes and dazzle her. She would be cold, like ice, like celadon. And if he wanted to possess her, he would pay the highest price.

He drank, filled his cup, and drank again, his eyes never leaving her face. Neither of them spoke. Finally he said abruptly, "Of course you will have to marry."

"I have no intention of marrying," Kaede replied, and then feared she had spoken too bluntly.

"I imagined you would say that, since you always hold a different opinion to the world. But in all practical terms you must be married. There is no alternative."

"My reputation is very unfavorable," Kaede said. "Too many men connected with me have perished. I do not want to be the cause of any more deaths."

She felt his interest deepen, noticed the curve of his mouth increase slightly. Yet, it was not with desire for her; she knew that. It was the same emotion she had caught a whiff of before: a burning curiosity, carefully controlled, to know all her secrets.

He called to Mamoru, telling him to send the servants away and retire himself.

"Where is your woman?" he said to Kaede. "Tell her to wait for you inside. I want to speak to you privately."

Kaede spoke to Shizuka. After a pause Fujiwara went on, "Are you warm enough? You must not be ill again. Ishida tells me you are prone to sudden fevers."

Of course, Ishida would tell him everything about me, Kaede thought as she replied, "Thank you, I am warm enough for the moment. But Lord Fujiwara will forgive me if I do not stay up long. I tire very easily."

"We will talk for a little while," he said. "We have many weeks before us, I hope—all winter, in fact. But there is something about this night, the snow, your presence here . . . it's a memory that will stay with us all our lives."

He wants to marry me, Kaede thought with a sense of shock, followed by deep unease. If he offered marriage, how could she refuse? To use his own phrase *in all practical terms,* it made perfect sense. It was a far greater honor than she deserved; it would solve all her problems of money and food; it was a highly desirable alliance. Yet, she knew his preference was for men; he neither loved nor desired her. She prayed he would not speak, for she did not see how she could refuse him. She was afraid of the strength of his will, which always took what it wanted and always had its own way. She doubted her own strength to deny him. Not only would it be an unthinkable insult to someone of his rank, but he fascinated her as much as he alarmed her and this gave him a power over her that she barely understood.

"I have never seen a bear," she said, hoping to change the subject, drawing the heavy skin closer around her.

"We have small bears here in the mountains; one came to the garden once after a particularly long winter. I had it captured and caged for a while, but it pined and died. It was nothing like this size. Ishida will tell us of his travels one day. Would you like that?"

"Very much. He is the only person I know who has ever been to the mainland."

"It's a dangerous voyage. Quite apart from the storms, there are often encounters with pirates."

At that moment, Kaede felt she would rather meet a dozen bears or twenty pirates than remain with this unnerving man. She could think of nothing else to say. Indeed, she felt powerless to move at all.

"Mamoru and Ishida have both told me what people say about you, that desire for you brings death."

Kaede said nothing. *I will not be ashamed*, she thought. *I have done nothing wrong.* She lifted her eyes and looked at him directly, her face calm, her gaze steady.

"Yet, from what Ishida tells me, one man who desired you escaped death."

She felt her heart twist and jump, like a fish when it finds its living flesh pierced by the cook's knife. His eyes flickered. A small muscle twitched in his cheek. He looked away from her at the snow. *He is asking what should not be asked,* she thought. *I will tell him, but he will pay a price for it.* As she saw his weakness, she became aware of her own power. Her courage began to return.

"Who was it?" he whispered.

The night was silent, apart from the soft drift of snow, the wind in the pines, the murmur of water.

"Lord Otori Takeo," she said.

"Yes, it could only be him," he replied, making her wonder what she had given away before and what he knew about Takeo now. He leaned forward, his face moving into the lamplight. "Tell me about it."

"I could tell you many things," she said slowly. "About Lord Shigeru's betrayal and death and Lord Takeo's revenge and what happened the night Iida died and Inuyama fell. But every story comes at a price. What will you give me in return?"

He smiled and in a tone of complicity said, "What does Lady Shirakawa desire?"

"I need money to hire men and equip them, and food for my household."

He came close to laughing. "Most women your age would ask for a new fan or a robe. But you are always able to surprise me."

"Do you accept my price?" She felt she had nothing to lose now from boldness.

"Yes, I do. For Iida, money; for Shigeru, bushels of rice. And for the living one—I assume he still lives—what shall I pay you for Takeo's story?"

His voice changed as he spoke the name, as though he were tasting it in his mouth, and she wondered again what he had heard about Takeo.

"Teach me," she said. "There are so many things I need to know. Teach me as if I were a boy."

He inclined his head in agreement. "It will be a pleasure to continue your father's instruction."

"But everything must be kept secret between us. Like the treasures of your collection, nothing must be exposed. I will divulge these things only for your gaze. No one else must ever be told them."

"That makes them all the more precious, all the more desirable."

"No one else has ever heard them," Kaede whispered. "And once I have told you, I will never speak of them again."

The wind had risen a little, and a flurry of snow blew onto the veranda, the flakes hissing as they hit the lamps and the braziers. Kaede could feel cold creeping over her, meeting her coldness of heart and spirit. She longed to leave him, yet knew she could not move until he released her.

"You are cold," he said, and clapped his hands. The servants appeared out of the shadows and helped Kaede to her feet, lifting the heavy fur from her.

"I look forward to your stories," he said, wishing her good night with unusual warmth. But Kaede found herself wondering if she had not made a pact with a demon from hell. She prayed he would not ask her to marry him. She would never allow him to cage her in this luxurious beautiful house, concealed like a treasure, to be gazed on only by him.

At the end of the week she returned home. The first

snow had melted and frozen, and the road was icy but passable. Icicles hung from the eaves of the houses, dripping in the sun, glistening and brilliant. Fujiwara had kept his word. He was a rigorous and demanding teacher and set her tasks to practice before she returned to his house again. He had already dispatched food for her household and men.

The days had been spent in study and the nights in storytelling. She knew by instinct what he wanted to hear, and she told him details she had not known she remembered: the color of flowers, the birds' song, the exact condition of the weather, the touch of a hand, the smell of a robe, the way lamplight fell on a face. And the undercurrents of desire and conspiracy that she had both known and not known, and that only now became clear to her with the telling. She told him everything, in a clear measured voice, showing neither shame, grief, nor regret.

He was reluctant to allow her to return home, but she used her sisters as an excuse. He wanted her to stay there forever, she knew, and she fought that desire silently. Yet, it seemed that everyone shared it. The servants expected it and their treatment of her changed slightly. They deferred to her as though she were already more than a specially favored guest. They sought her permission, her opinion, and she knew they would only do so if he had so ordered.

She felt deep relief when she left him and she dreaded returning again. But when she was home, she saw the food, the firewood, and the money he had sent, and was grateful that he had kept her family from starving. That night she lay thinking, *I am trapped. I shall never escape him. Yet what else can I do?*

It was a long time before she slept, and she was late rising the next morning. Shizuka was not in the room when she awoke. Kaede called to her, and Ayame came in with tea.

She poured Kaede a cup. "Shizuka is with Kondo," she said. "He returned late last night."

"Tell her to come to me," Kaede said. She looked at the tea as though she did not know what to do with it. She sipped a mouthful, placed the cup on the tray, then picked it up. Her hands were icy. She held the cup between them, trying to warm them.

"Lord Fujiwara sent this tea," Ayame said. "A whole box of it. Isn't it delicious?"

"Fetch Shizuka!" Kaede cried angrily. "Tell her to come to me at once!"

A few minutes later Shizuka came into the room and knelt in front of Kaede. Her face was somber.

"What is it?" Kaede asked, "Is he dead?" The cup began to shake in her hands, spilling the tea.

Shizuka took it from her and held her hands tightly. "You must not be distressed. You must not become ill. He is not dead. But he has left the Tribe, and they have issued an edict against him."

"What does that mean?"

"You remember what he told you at Terayama? If he did not go with them, they would not allow him to live. It is the same."

"Why?" Kaede said. "Why? I don't understand."

"It's the way the Tribe are. Obedience is everything to them."

"So why would he leave them?"

"It's not clear. There was some altercation, some disagreement. He was sent on a mission and never came back from it." Shizuka paused. "Kondo thinks he may be at Terayama. If he is, he will be safe there for the winter."

Kaede pulled her hands away from Shizuka and stood. "I must go there."

"It's impossible," Shizuka said. "It's already closed off by snow."

"I must see him!" Kaede said, her eyes blazing in her pale face. "If he has left the Tribe, he will become Otori again. If he is Otori, we can marry!"

"Lady!" Shizuka stood, too. "What madness is this? You cannot just take after him like that! Even if the roads were open it would be unthinkable. Better, by far, to marry Fujiwara, if you want what you say you want. It is what he desires."

Kaede struggled to regain control of herself. "There is nothing to stop me from going to Terayama. Indeed, I should go there . . . on a pilgrimage . . . to give thanks to the all-merciful one for saving my life. I have promised to go to Inuyama, to Arai, as soon as the snows melt. I shall go to the temple the way. Even if Lord Fujiwara does want to marry me, I can do nothing without consulting Lord Arai. Oh, Shizuka, how long is it till spring?"

· 4 ·

The winter days crawled past. Every month Kaede went to Lord Fujiwara's residence, stayed for a week, and recounted the story of her life, at night while the snow fell or the moon shone coldly on the frozen garden. He asked many questions and made her repeat many parts.

"It could be the subject of a drama," he said more than once. "Maybe I should try my hand at writing such a thing."

"You would never be able to show it to anyone," she replied.

"No, the delight would be in the writing alone. I would share it with you, of course. We might have it acted once for our pleasure and then have the actors put to death."

He often made comments like this, with no trace of emotion, alarming her more and more, though she kept her fears hidden. With each retelling her face became more masklike, her movements more studied, as though she were endlessly acting out her life on a stage he had created as carefully as the perfectly constructed theater where Mamoru and the other young men played their roles.

During the day he kept his promise to teach her as if she were a boy. He used men's language with her and made her speak it to him. It amused him sometimes to see her dressed in Mamoru's clothes, with her hair tied back. The role-playing exhausted her. But she learned.

Fujiwara kept his other promises, having food delivered to her house and money handed over to Shizuka at the end of each visit. Kaede counted it with the same avidity with which she studied. She saw them both as equal currency for her future, giving her freedom and power.

In early spring there was a bitter snap of cold weather that froze the plum blossoms on the branches. Kaede's impatience grew with the lengthening days; the increased cold and harder frosts, followed by fresh snow, nearly drove her mad. She could feel her mind, frantic like a bird trapped inside the house; yet, she did not dare share her feelings with anyone, not even with Shizuka.

On sunny days she went to the stables and watched Raku when Amano let the horses out to gallop in the water meadows. The horse often seemed to look questioningly toward the northeast, tasting the sharp wind.

"Soon," she promised him. "Soon we will be on our way."

Finally the full moon of the third month turned and brought with it a warm wind from the south. Kaede woke to the sound of water dripping from the eaves, trickling through the garden, racing down the waterfalls. In three days the snow was gone. The world lay bare and muddy, waiting to be filled with sound and color again.

"I have to go away for a while," she told Fujiwara on her last visit. "I have been summoned by Lord Arai to Inuyama."

"You will seek his permission to marry?"

"It is something that must be discussed with him before I can make any decisions," she murmured.

"Then I will let you go." His lips curved slightly but the smile did not reach his eyes.

For the last month she had been making preparations, waiting for the thaw, thankful for Fujiwara's money. Within a week she left on a cold, bright morning, the sun appearing and disappearing behind racing clouds, the wind from the east, keen and bracing. Hana had begged to be allowed to come, and at first Kaede intended to take her. But a fear grew in her that once they were at Inuyama, Arai might keep her sister as a hostage. For the time being, Hana was safer at home. She hardly admitted even to herself that if Takeo were at Terayama, she might never go on to the capital. Ai did not want to come, and Kaede left her hostage, Mitsuru, with Shoji, as a guarantee for her own safety.

She took Kondo, Amano, and six other men. She wanted to move quickly, always aware of how short a life might be and how precious every hour was. She put on men's garments and rode Raku. He had wintered well, hardly losing any weight, and he stepped out with an eagerness that equaled hers. He was already shedding his winter coat, and the rough gray hair clung to her clothes.

Shizuka accompanied her, along with one of the maids from the house, Manami. Shizuka had decided she would go at least as far as Terayama and, while Kaede went on to the capital, she would visit her grandparents' home, in the mountains behind Yamagata, to see her sons. Manami was a sensible and practical woman who quickly took it upon herself to supervise their meals and lodging at the inns along the road, demanding hot food and water, disputing prices, cowing innkeepers, and always getting her own way.

"I won't have to worry about who'll look after you when I leave you," Shizuka said on the third night, after hearing Manami scold the innkeeper for providing inferior, flea-ridden bedding. "I think Manami's tongue would stop an ogre in its tracks."

"I'll miss you," Kaede said. "I think you are my courage. I don't know how brave I can be without you. And who will tell me what is really happening beneath all the lies and the pretense?"

"I think you can discern that well enough for yourself," Shizuka replied. "Besides, Kondo will be with you. You will make a better impression on Arai without me!"

"What should I expect from Arai?"

"He has always taken your part. He will continue to champion you. He is generous and loyal, except when he feels he has been slighted or deceived."

"He is impulsive, I thought," Kaede said.

"Yes, to the point of rashness. He is hot in every sense of the word, passionate and stubborn."

"You loved him very much?" Kaede said.

"I was only a girl. He was my first lover. I was deeply in love with him, and he must have loved me after his own fashion. He kept me with him for fourteen years."

"I will plead with him to forgive you," Kaede exclaimed.

"I don't know which I fear most, his forgiveness or his rage," Shizuka admitted, thinking of Dr. Ishida and the discreet, entirely satisfactory affair they had been conducting all winter.

"Then maybe I should not mention you at all."

"It's usually better to say nothing," Shizuka agreed. "Anyway, his main concern will be with your marriage and the alliances that may be made by it."

"I will not marry until I have secured Maruyama," Kaede replied. "First he must assist me in that."

But first I must see Takeo, she thought. *If he is not at Terayama, I will forget him. It will be a sign that it is not meant to be. Oh, merciful heaven, let him be there!*

As the road ascended farther into the mountain range,

the thaw was less apparent. Drifts of unmelted snow still covered the paths in places, and often there was ice underfoot. The horses' feet were wrapped in straw, but their progress was slow and Kaede's impatience intensified.

Finally, late one afternoon, they arrived at the inn at the foot of the holy mountain where Kaede had rested when she had first visited the temple with Lady Maruyama. Here they would stay the night before making the final ascent the next day.

Kaede slept fitfully, her mind full of the companions from her previous journey whose names were now entered in the ledgers of the dead. She recalled the day they had ridden out together, how lighthearted everyone had seemed while they had been planning assassination and civil war. She had known nothing of that; she had been a green girl nursing a secret love. She felt a wave of scornful pity for that innocent, guileless self. She had changed completely, but the love had not changed.

The light was paling behind the shutters, and birds were calling. The room seemed unbearably stuffy. Manami was snoring slightly. Kaede got up quietly, pulled on a quilted robe, and slid open the door to the courtyard. From behind the wall she could hear the horses stamping on their lines. She heard one of them give a whicker of recognition. *The men must be up already,* she thought, and heard footsteps turn through the gate. She stepped behind the shutter again.

Everything was misty and indistinct in the dawn light. A figure came into the courtyard. She thought, *It's him.* She thought, *It cannot be.*

Takeo came out of the mist toward her.

She stepped onto the veranda, and as he recognized her she saw the look that swept across his face. She thought, with gratitude and relief, *It's all right. He's alive. He loves me.*

He came up onto the veranda silently and fell on his knees before her. She knelt too. "Sit up," she whispered.

He did so, and they stared at each other for several moments, she as if she would drink him in, he obliquely, not meeting her gaze. They sat awkwardly, so much between them.

Takeo said finally, "I saw my horse. I knew you must be here, but I couldn't believe it."

"I heard you were here. In great danger, but alive."

"The danger is not so great," he said. "My greatest danger is from you—that you cannot forgive me."

"I can't *not* forgive you," she replied simply. "As long as you don't leave me again."

"I was told you were to be married. I have been afraid of it all winter."

"There is someone who wants to marry me: Lord Fujiwara. But we are not married yet, not even betrothed."

"Then we must marry immediately. Are you here to visit the temple?"

"That was my intention. Then I was to go on to Inuyama." She was studying his face. He looked older, the bones more pronounced, the mouth more determined. His hair, shorter than it had been, was not pulled back in the warrior style but fell against his forehead, thick and glossy.

"I'll send men to escort you up the mountain. I'll come to the women's rooms in the temple this evening. We have so much to plan. Don't look in my eyes," he added. "I don't want you to fall asleep."

"I don't mind," she replied. "Sleep rarely comes to me. Send me to sleep until this evening, then the hours will pass quickly. When I slept before, the White Goddess came to me in a vision. She told me to be patient, to wait for you. I am here to thank her for it and for saving my life."

"I was told you were dying," he said, and could not continue. After a few moments he spoke with an effort. "Is Muto Shizuka with you?"

"Yes."

"And you have a retainer from the Tribe, Kondo Kiichi?"

She nodded.

"They must be sent away. Leave your other men here for the time being. Do you have another woman to accompany you?"

"Yes," Kaede said. "But I don't think Shizuka would do anything to harm you." Even as she spoke, she thought, *But how do I know? Can I trust Shizuka? Or Kondo, come to that. I have seen his ruthlessness.*

"I am under sentence of death from the Tribe," Takeo said. "Therefore any one of them is a danger to me."

"Isn't it dangerous for you to be out like this?"

He smiled. "I've never let anyone confine me. I like to explore places at night. I need to know the terrain, and if the Otori are planning to attack me across the border. I was on my way back when I saw Raku. He recognized me. Did you hear him?"

"He has been waiting for you, too," she said, and felt

sorrow uncurl in her belly. "Does everyone want your death?"

"They are not going to succeed. Not yet. I'll tell you why tonight."

She longed for him to hold her. She could feel her body leaning toward him. In the same moment he responded and took her in his arms. She felt his heart beat, his lips against her neck. Then he whispered, "Someone's awake. I must go."

She could hear nothing. Takeo pulled gently away from her. "Till this evening," he said.

She looked at him, seeking his gaze, half hoping to be plunged into sleep, but he had gone. She cried out in alarm. There was no sign of him in the courtyard or beyond. The wind chimes rang out sharply as if in the breath of someone passing beneath them. Her heart was pounding. Had it been his ghost that had come to her? Had she been dreaming, and what would she find when she awoke?

"What are you doing out here, lady?" Manami's voice was shrill with concern. "You'll catch your death of cold."

Kaede pulled the robe around her. She was indeed shivering. "I could not sleep," she said slowly. "I had a dream. . . ."

"Go inside. I'll send for tea." Manami stepped into her sandals and hurried away across the courtyard.

Swallows darted to and from the eaves. Kaede smelled wood smoke as the fires were lit. The horses whinnied as they were fed. She heard Raku's voice as she had heard it earlier. The air was sharp, but she could smell blossoms. She felt her heart swell with hope. It had not been a dream. He was here. In a few hours they would be together. She did not want to go inside. She wanted to stay where she was, remembering his look, his touch, his smell.

Manami came back, carrying a tray with tea and cups on it. She scolded Kaede again, and chivied her into the room. Shizuka was getting dressed. She took one look at Kaede and exclaimed, "You've seen Takeo?"

Kaede did not reply immediately. She took a cup of tea from Manami and drank it slowly. She felt she had to be careful what she said: Shizuka was from the Tribe, who had placed Takeo under sentence of death. She had assured Takeo that Shizuka would not harm him, but how could she be certain of that? However, she found she could not control her expression, could not stop smiling, as if the mask had cracked and fallen away.

"I am going to the temple," she said. "I must get ready. Manami will come with me. Shizuka, you may leave now to see your sons, and you can take Kondo with you."

"I thought Kondo was to go with you to Inuyama," Shizuka said.

"I have changed my mind. He must go with you. And you must both leave at once, now."

"These are Takeo's orders, I suppose," Shizuka said. "You cannot pretend to me. I know you have seen him."

"I told him you would not harm him," Kaede said. "You would not?"

Shizuka said sharply, "Better not to ask that. If I do not see him, I cannot harm him. But how long do you intend to stay at the temple? Don't forget, Arai is waiting for you at Inuyama."

"I don't know. It all depends on Takeo." Kaede could not prevent herself from continuing. "He said we must marry. We must; we will."

"You must not do anything before you have seen Arai," Shizuka said urgently. "If you marry without his approval, you will insult him. He will be deeply offended. You cannot afford to incite his enmity. He is your strongest ally. And what about Lord Fujiwara? You are as good as betrothed to him. Will you offend him, too?"

"I cannot marry Fujiwara," Kaede cried. "He of all people knows that I can marry no one but Takeo. To all other men I bring death. But I am Takeo's life and he is mine."

"This is not the way the world works," Shizuka said. "Remember what Lady Maruyama told you, how easily these warlords and warriors can crush a woman if they think that you question their power over you. Fujiwara expects to marry you: He must have already consulted Arai. It is a match Arai can only be in favor of. Apart from that, Takeo has the entire Tribe against him; he cannot survive. Don't look at me like that: It distresses me to hurt you. It's because I care so much for you that I must say this to you. I could swear to you never to harm him, but it would make no difference; there are hundreds out there who will try. Sooner or later one of them will succeed. No one can escape the Tribe forever. You have to accept that this will be his fate. What will you do after his death, when you have insulted everyone who takes your part? You will have no hope of Maruyama and will lose Shirakawa. Your sisters will be ruined with you. Arai is your overlord. You must go to Inuyama and accept his decision on your marriage. Otherwise you will enrage him. Believe me: I know how his mind works."

"Can Arai prevent the coming of spring?" Kaede replied. "Can he order the snow not to thaw?"

"All men like to believe they can. Women get their own way by indulging this belief, not by opposing it."

"Lord Arai will learn differently," Kaede said in a low voice. "Make yourself ready. You and Kondo must be gone in an hour."

She turned away. Her heart was beating wildly, excitement building up in her belly, her chest, her throat. She could think of nothing other than being joined with him. The sight of him, his closeness, awoke the fever in her again.

"You are mad," Shizuka said. "You have gone beyond reason. You are unleashing disaster on yourself and your family."

As if in confirmation of Shizuka's fears, there was a sudden noise; the house groaned, the screens rattled, the wind chimes sounded as the ground shook beneath their feet.

· 5 ·

As soon as the snow began to melt and the thaw came, word spread like running water that I was at Terayama and was going to challenge the Otori lords for my inheritance. And like running water, first in a trickle, then in a flood, warriors began to make their way to the mountain temple. Some were masterless, but most were Otori who recognized the legitimacy of my claim as Shigeru's heir. My story was already a legend, and I seemed to have become a hero, not only to the young men of the warrior class, but also to the farmers and villagers of the Otori domain, who had reached a state of desperation after the bitter winter, the increased taxation, and the ever-harsher laws imposed by Shoichi and Masahiro, Shigeru's uncles.

The air was full of the sounds of spring. The willows put on their gold-green fronds. Swallows darted over the flooded fields and crafted their nests under the eaves of the temple buildings. Every night the noise of frogs grew louder, the loud call of the rain frog, the clacking rhythm of the tree frog, and the sweet tinkling of the little bell frog. Flowers bloomed in a riot along the dikes: bitter cress, buttercups, and bright pink vetch. Herons, ibis, and cranes returned to the rivers and the pools.

The abbot, Matsuda Shingen, made the considerable wealth of the temple freely available to me, and with his help I spent the early weeks of spring organizing the men who came to me, equipping and arming them. Smiths and armorers appeared from Yamagata and elsewhere and set up their workshops at the foot of the holy mountain. Every day horse dealers came, hoping to make a good sale, and they usually did, for I bought all the horses I could. No matter how many men I had and how well they were armed, my main weapons would always be speed and surprise. I did not have the time or the resources to muster a huge army of foot soldiers like Arai. I had to rely on a small but swifter band of horsemen.

Among the first to arrive were the Miyoshi brothers, Kahei and Gemba, with whom I had trained in Hagi. Those days when we had fought with wooden swords now seemed impossibly distant. Their appearance meant a great deal to me, far more than they suspected when they fell to their knees and begged to be allowed to join me. It meant that the best of the Otori had not forgotten Shigeru. They brought thirty men with them and, just as welcome, news from Hagi.

"Shoichi and Masahiro are aware of your return," Kahei told me. He was several years older than me and had some experience of war, having been at Yaegahara at the age of fourteen. "But they don't take it very seriously. They feel it will only take one quick skirmish to rout you." He grinned at me. "I don't mean to insult you, but they've formed the impression that you're something of a weakling."

"That's the only way they've seen me," I replied. I remembered Iida's retainer, Abe, who had thought the same thing and had been taught differently by Jato. "They are correct in some ways. It is true that I am young and know only the theory of war, not its practice. But I have right on my side and am fulfilling Shigeru's will."

"People say you are touched by heaven," Gemba said.

"They say you have been given powers that are not of this world."

"We know all about that!" said Kahei. "Remember the fight with Yoshitomi? But he considered the powers to be from hell, not heaven."

I had fought a bout against Masahiro's son with wooden swords. He was a better swordsman than I was then, but I had other skills that he thought cheating and I had used them to prevent him from killing me.

"Have they taken my house and land?" I asked. "I heard they intended to."

"Not yet, mainly because our old teacher, Ichiro, has refused to hand them over. He's made it clear he won't give in without a fight. The lords are reluctant to start a brawl with him and Shigeru's—your—remaining men."

It was a relief to me to know that Ichiro was still alive. I hoped he would leave soon and come to the temple, where I could protect him. Since the thaw I had been expecting him daily.

"Also, they are not certain of the townspeople," Gemba put in. "They don't want to provoke anyone. They're afraid of an uprising."

"They always preferred to plot in secret," I said.

"They call it negotiation," Kahei said dryly. "Have they tried to negotiate with you?"

"I've heard nothing from them. Besides, there is nothing to negotiate. They were responsible for Shigeru's death. They tried to murder him in his own house, and when that failed they handed him over to Iida. I cannot come to an agreement with them, even if they offer it."

"What will be your strategy?" Kahei asked, narrowing his eyes.

"There's no way I can attack the Otori in Hagi. I'd need far greater resources than I have now. I am thinking I must approach Arai . . . but I'll do nothing until Ichiro gets here. He said he would come as soon as the road was clear."

"Send us to Inuyama," Kahei said. "Our mother's sister is married to one of Arai's retainers. We can find out if winter has changed Arai's attitude toward you."

"When the time is right, I will," I promised, glad to have a way to approach Arai indirectly. I did not tell them or anyone yet what I had already decided: to go first to Kaede, wherever she was, and marry her and then to take over the Shirakawa and Maruyama lands with her, if she would still have me, if she was not already married. . . .

With every spring day my restlessness increased. The weather was fickle, sun one day, icy winds the next. The plum trees blossomed in a hailstorm. Even when the cherry buds started to swell, it was still cold. But there were signs of spring everywhere—especially, it seemed, in my blood. The disciplined life of the past winter had left me fitter than I had ever been, physically and mentally. Matsuda's teaching, his unfailing affection for me, the knowledge of my Otori blood had all given me new self-confidence. I was less ridden by my split nature, less troubled by conflicting loyalties. I made no outward show of the restlessness that tormented me. I was learning to show nothing to the world. But at night my thoughts turned to Kaede, and my desire followed. I longed for her, fearing that she was married to someone else and lost to me forever. When I could not sleep I slipped from the room and left the temple, exploring the surrounding district, sometimes going as far as Yamagata. The hours of meditation, study, and training had honed all my skills; I had no fear of anyone detecting me.

Makoto and I met every day to study together, but by silent agreement we did not touch each other. Our friendship had moved onto another plane, which I felt would last a life-time. Nor did I sleep with any women. None was allowed in the temple itself, fears of assassination kept me from the brothels, and I did not want to start another child. I often thought of Yuki. I could not stop myself from passing in front of her parents' house one moonless night late in the second month. The plum tree's blossoms gleamed white in the darkness, but there were no lights within and only one guard on the gate. I'd heard that Arai's men had ransacked the house in the autumn. Now it seemed to be deserted. Even the smell of the fermenting soybeans had faded.

I thought about our child. I was sure it would be a boy, brought up by the Tribe to hate me and in all probability des-tined to fulfill the blind woman's prophecy. Knowing the future did not mean that I could escape it: It was part of the bitter sadness of human life.

I wondered where Yuki was now—possibly in some distant secret village north of Matsue—and I often thought about her father, Kenji. He probably would be not so far away, in one of the Muto villages in the mountains, not knowing that the secret network of the Tribe's hiding places had all been revealed to me in the records that Shigeru had left and that I had spent the winter learning by heart. I was still not sure what I would do with this knowledge: whether I would take advantage of it to buy forgiveness and friendship from Arai, or use it myself to eradicate the secret organization that had sentenced me to death.

A long time ago Kenji had sworn to protect me as long as I lived. I discounted this promise as part of the deviousness of his nature, and I had not forgiven him for his part in Shigeru's betrayal. But I also knew that without him I would not have been able to carry out the work of revenge, and I could not forget that he had followed me back into the castle that night. If I could have chosen anyone's help, it would have been his, but I did not think he would ever go against the rulings of the Tribe. If we met it would be as enemies, each seeking to kill the other.

Once when I was coming home at dawn I heard an animal's sharp panting and surprised a wolf on the path. He could smell me but could not see me. I was close enough to see the bright reddish hair behind his ears, close enough to smell his breath. He snarled in fear, backed away, turned, and slipped into the undergrowth. I could hear him stop and sniff again, his nose as sharp as my ears. Our worlds of the senses overlapped, mine dominated by hearing, his by smell. I wondered what it would be like to enter the wolf's wild and solitary realm. In the Tribe I was known as the Dog, but I preferred to think of myself like this wolf, no longer owned by anyone.

Then the morning came when I saw my horse, Raku. It was late in the third month, when the cherry blossoms were on the point of flowering. I was walking up the steep track as the sky lightened, my eyes on the mountain peaks, still snow-covered, turning pink in the sun. I saw the unfamiliar horses on their lines outside the inn. No one seemed to be up, though I heard a shutter slide open from the other side of the courtyard. My gaze drifted over the horses as it always does, and at the same time as I recognized Raku's gray coat and black mane, the horse turned his head, saw me, and whickered in delight.

He had been my gift to Kaede; he was almost my only possession left after the fall of Inuyama. Could she have sold him or given him away? Or had he brought her here to me?

Between the stables and the guest rooms of the inn was a small courtyard, with pine trees and stone lanterns. I stepped into it. I knew someone was awake; I could hear breathing behind the shutters. I went toward the veranda, desperate to know if it was Kaede, and at the same time certain that in the next moment I would see her.

She was even lovelier than I remembered. Her illness had left her thinner and frailer, but it had brought out the beauty of her bones, the slenderness of her wrists and neck. The pounding of my heart silenced the world around me. Then, realizing that for a few moments we would be alone before the inn awoke, I went and knelt before her.

All too soon I heard the women wake inside the room. I took on invisibility and slipped away. I heard Kaede's gasp of fear and realized I had not yet told her about my Tribe skills. There was so much we needed to talk about: Would we ever have enough time? The wind chimes rang out as I passed beneath them. I could see my horse looking for me, but he did not see me. Then my shape returned. I was striding up the hill, filled with energetic joy as if I had drunk some magic potion. Kaede was here. She was not married. She would be mine.

As I did every day, I went to the burial ground and knelt before Shigeru's grave. At this early hour it was deserted, the light dim beneath the cedars. The sun was touching their tips; on the opposite side of the valley the mist hung along the sides of the slopes, so the peaks seemed to be floating on foam.

The waterfall kept up its ceaseless babble, echoed by the softer trickle of water flowing through gutters and pipes into the pools and cisterns of the garden. I could hear the monks at prayer, the rise and fall of the sutras, the sudden clear peal of a bell. I was glad Shigeru dwelled in this peaceful place. I spoke to his spirit, asking for his strength and wisdom to be transferred to me. I told him what he no doubt already knew: that I was going to fulfill his last requests to me. And, first of all, I was going to marry Shirakawa Kaede.

There was a sudden heavy shaking as the earth trembled. I was gripped by certainty that I was doing the right thing, and also by a sense of urgency. We must marry immediately.

A change in the note of the water made me turn my head. In the large pond, carp were threshing and milling just below the surface of the water, a flickering mat of red and gold. Makoto was feeding them, his face calm and serene as he watched them.

Red and gold filled my eyes, the colors of good fortune, the colors of marriage.

He saw me looking at him and called, "Where were you? You missed the first meal."

"I'll eat later." I got to my feet and went toward him. I could not keep my excitement to myself. "Lady Shirakawa is here. Will you go with Kahei and escort her to the women's guest house?"

He threw the last of the millet into the water. "I will tell Kahei. I prefer not to go myself. I don't want to remind her of the pain I caused her."

"Maybe you are right. Yes, tell Kahei. Let them bring her here before noon."

"Why is she here?" Makoto asked, glancing sideways at me.

"She came on a pilgrimage, to give thanks for her recovery. But now that she is here, I intend to marry her."

"Just like that?" He laughed without mirth.

"Why not?"

"My experience of marriages is very limited, but I believe in the case of great families like the Shirakawa or, come to that, the Otori, consent has to be given: The clan lords have to agree."

"I am the lord of my clan and I give my consent," I

replied lightly, feeling he was raising unnecessary problems.

"Your case is slightly different. But who does Lady Shirakawa obey? Her family may have other plans for her."

"She has no family." I could feel anger beginning to simmer.

"Don't be a fool, Takeo. Everyone has family, especially unmarried girls who are the heir to great domains."

"I have both legal right and moral duty to marry her, since she was betrothed to my adopted father." My tone was hotter now. "It was Shigeru's express will that I should do so."

"Don't be angry with me," he said, after a pause. "I know your feelings for her. I'm only saying what everyone will tell you."

"She loves me too!"

"Love has nothing to do with marriage." He shook his head, looking at me as if I were a child.

"Nothing's going to stop me! She is here. I will not let her slip away from me again. We will be married this week."

The bell tolled from the temple. One of the older monks walked across the garden, looking disapprovingly at us. Makoto had kept his voice low throughout our exchange, but I had been talking loudly and forcefully.

"I must go to meditation," he said. "Maybe you should too. Think about what you are doing before you act."

"My mind is made up. Go and meditate! I'll tell Kahei. And then I'll speak to the abbot."

It was already past the time when I usually went to him every morning for two hours of swordsmanship. I hurried to find the Miyoshi brothers, and caught up with them on their way downhill to speak to an armorer.

"Lady Shirakawa?" Kahei said. "Is it safe to go near her?"

"Why do you say that?" I demanded.

"No offense, Takeo, but everyone knows about her. She brings death to men."

"Only if they desire her," Gemba added; then, taking a quick look at my face, he went on, "That's what people say!"

"And they also say that she's so beautiful, it's impossible to look at her without desiring her." Kahei looked gloomy. "You're sending us to certain death."

I was in no mood for their clowning, but their words brought home to me even more how essential it was that we should marry. Kaede had said that she was safe only with me, and I understood why: Only marriage to me would save her from the curse she seemed to be under. I knew that she would never be any danger to me. Other men who desired her had died, but I had joined my body to hers and lived.

I was not going to explain all this to the Miyoshi brothers.

"Bring her to the women's guest rooms as soon as possible," I said shortly. "Make sure none of her men come and also that Kondo Kiichi and Muto Shizuka leave today. She will bring one woman with her. Treat them with the utmost courtesy. Tell her I will call on her around the hour of the Monkey."

"Takeo is truly fearless," Gemba muttered.

"Lady Shirakawa is going to be my wife."

That startled them. They saw I was serious and kept their mouths closed. They bowed formally to me and walked silently to the guardhouse, where they collected five or six other men. Once they were beyond the gate, they made a few jokes at my expense, not realizing that I could hear them, about the praying mantis that devours her mate. I thought about going after them to teach them a lesson, but I was already late for the abbot.

Listening to their laughter fade away down the slope, I hurried to the hall where our sessions took place. He was already there, dressed in his priest's robes. I was still in the rough garb I wore on my nighttime wanderings; a sort of adaptation of the Tribe's black uniform: knee-length trousers, leggings, and split-toed boots that did as well for sword fighting as for leaping up walls and running over roofs.

Matsuda did not seem to be at all encumbered by his long skirts and deep sleeves. I usually finished the sessions out of breath and pouring with sweat. He remained as cool and unruffled as if he had spent those same two hours in prayer.

I knelt before him to apologize for my lateness. He looked me up and down, a quizzical expression on his face, but said nothing, indicating the wooden pole with his head.

I took it from the rack. It was dark in color, almost black, longer than Jato and much heavier. Since I had been practicing daily with it, the muscles in my wrists and arms had increased in strength and flexibility, and I finally seemed to be over the injury to my right hand that Akio had caused me in Inuyama. At first the pole had felt like an obstinate horse, slugging against the bit; little by little I had learned to control it until I could manipulate it as deftly as a pair of eating sticks.

In practice that precision was as necessary as in real

combat, for a false move could crack a skull or crush a breast-bone. We did not have enough men to risk killing or injuring each other in training.

A wave of tiredness swept over me as I raised the pole into the challenge position. I had barely slept the night before and had not eaten since the evening meal. Then I thought of Kaede, saw her form as I'd seen her earlier, kneeling on the veranda. Energy flowed back into me. I realized in that split second how completely necessary she was to me.

Normally I was no match for Matsuda. But something had transformed me, had taken all the elements of training and melded them into a whole: a tough, indestructible spirit that sprang from the core of my being and flowed into my sword arm. For the first time I realized I was forty years younger than Matsuda. I saw his age and his vulnerability. I saw I had him at my mercy.

I checked my attack and let the pole drop. In that instant his staff found the unguarded space, catching me on the side of the neck with a blow that left me dizzy. Luckily he had not struck with full force.

His normally serene eyes were blazing with genuine anger.

"That's to teach you a lesson," he growled. "First, not to

be late and, second, not to let your softness of heart emerge while you're fighting."

I opened my mouth to speak but he cut me off. "Don't argue. You give me the first inkling I'm not wasting my time with you and then you throw it away. Why? Not because you felt pity for me, I hope?"

I shook my head.

He sighed. "You can't fool me. I saw it in your eyes. I saw the boy who came here last year and was moved by Sesshu. Is that what you want to be? An artist? I told you then that you could come back here and study and draw. Is that what you want?"

I was disinclined to answer but he waited until I did. "A part of me might want it, but not yet. First I have to carry out Shigeru's commands."

"Are you sure of that? Will you commit yourself to it with a whole heart?"

I heard the utter seriousness of his tone and answered in the same way. "Yes, I will."

"You will be leading many men, some to their death. Are you sure enough of yourself to do that? If you have any weakness, Takeo, it is this: You feel too much pity. A warrior needs more than a dash of ruthlessness, of black blood. Many will die following you, and you will kill many yourself. Once you launch yourself on this path, you must pursue it to the end. You cannot check your attack or drop your guard because you feel pity for your opponent."

I could feel the color mounting to my face. "I will not do it again. I did not mean to insult you. Forgive me."

"I'll forgive you if you can achieve that move again and follow it through!"

He took up the challenge position, his eyes fixed on mine. I had no qualms about meeting his gaze: He had never succumbed to the Kikuta sleep, and I had never tried to impose it on him. Nor did I ever intentionally use invisibility or the second self with him, though sometimes, in the heat of combat, I felt my image begin to slide away.

His staff moved like lightning through the air. I stopped thinking then about anything except the opponent in front of me and the thrust of the pole, the floor beneath our feet, the space around us that we filled almost like a dance. And twice more I came to the same point where I saw my dominance over him, and neither time did I fail to follow the move through.

When we had finished, even Matsuda was glowing slightly, perhaps due to the spring weather. As we were wiping the sweat from our faces with towels Norio brought, he said, "I did not think you would ever make a swordsman, but you have done better than I expected. When you concentrate you are not bad, not bad at all."

I was speechless at such high praise. He laughed. "Don't let it go to your head. I'll meet you again later this afternoon. I hope you have prepared your study on strategy."

"Yes, sir. But there is something else I need to talk to you about."

"Something to do with Lady Shirakawa?"

"How did you know?"

"I'd already heard that she was on her way to visit the temple. Arrangements have been made for her to stay in the women's guest house. It is a great honor for us. I will go and see her later today."

It all sounded like casual chat about an ordinary guest, but I knew Matsuda well enough by now: He did nothing casually. I was afraid he would have the same misgivings about my marriage to Kaede that Makoto had voiced, but I had to tell him my intentions sooner or later. All this flashed through my head in an instant, and then it occurred to me that if I should seek anyone's permission, it should be his.

I fell to my knees and said, "I wish to marry Lady Shirakawa. May I have your permission and may the ceremony be held here?"

"Is that the reason she came here? Does she come with the permission of her family and clan?"

"No, she came for a different purpose: to give thanks for recovering from an illness. But it was one of Lord Shigeru's last commands to me that I should marry her, and now fate seems to have brought her here to me. . . ." I heard a note of pleading in my voice.

The abbot heard it too. Smiling, he said, "The problem is not going to be on your side, Takeo. For you it is the right thing to do. But for her to marry without approval from her clan, from Lord Arai . . . Be patient, seek his permission. He was in favor of the marriage last year. There's every reason to think he still will be."

"I may be murdered at any moment!" I exclaimed. "I have no time to be patient! And there is someone else who wishes to marry her."

"Are they betrothed?"

"There is nothing official. But apparently he has expectations of the marriage taking place. He is a nobleman; his estate lies alongside hers."

"Fujiwara," Matsuda said.

"You know him?"

"I know who he is. Everyone does, apart from half-literates like you. It's a very suitable alliance. The estates will be joined, Fujiwara's son will inherit them both, and more important, since Fujiwara will almost certainly return to the capital soon, Arai will have a friend at court."

"Arai will not, because she will not marry Fujiwara. She will marry me, and before the end of the week!"

"Between them they will crush you." His eyes were fixed on my face.

"Not if Arai thinks I can help him destroy the Tribe. And when we marry we will move at once to Maruyama. Lady Shirakawa is the legal heir to that domain as well as to her father's. It will give me the resources I need to challenge the Otori."

"As a strategy, it's not bad," he said. "But there are grave risks: You could completely antagonize Arai. I'd thought it better for you to serve under him for a while and learn the art

242

of war. And you do not want to make an enemy of a man like Fujiwara. This move, for all its boldness, could destroy your hopes utterly. I don't want to see that happen. I want to see all of Shigeru's desires fulfilled. Is it worth the gamble?"

"Nothing will prevent me from marrying her," I said in a low voice.

"You are infatuated with her. Don't let that affect your judgment."

"It's more than infatuation: She is my life and I am hers."

He sighed. "We all think that at some age about some woman or other. Believe me, it doesn't last."

"Lord Shigeru and Lady Maruyama loved each other deeply for years," I dared to say.

"Yes, well, it must be some madness in the Otori blood," he retorted, but his expression had softened and his eyes took on a musing look.

"It's true," he said finally. "Their love did last. And it illuminated all their plans and hopes. If they had married, and brought about the alliance they dreamed of between the Middle Country and the West, who knows what they might not have achieved?" He reached down and patted me on the shoulder. "It's as if their spirits have brought about a second chance in you and Lady Shirakawa. And I can't deny it: To make Maruyama your base makes a great deal of sense. For that reason, as much as for the sake of the dead, I will agree to this marriage. You may start making the necessary preparations."

"I've never been to this sort of wedding," I confessed after I had bowed to the ground in gratitude. "What needs to be done?"

"The woman that came with her will know. Ask her. I hope I haven't reached my dotage," he added before dismissing me.

It was nearly time for the midday meal. I went to wash and change my clothes. I dressed with care, putting on another of the silk robes with the Otori crest on the back that had been given to me when I arrived at Terayama after my journey through the snow. I ate distractedly, hardly tasting the food, listening all the time for her arrival.

Finally I heard Kahei's voice outside the eating hall. I called to him and he came in to join me.

"Lady Shirakawa is at the women's guest rooms," he said. "Fifty more men have come from Hagi. We'll billet them in the village. Gemba is arranging it."

"I'll see them tonight," I said, my heart lifting from both pieces of news. I left him eating and went back to my room, where I knelt at the writing table and took out the scrolls the abbot had told me to read. I thought I would die of impatience before I saw Kaede again, but gradually I became absorbed in the art of war: the accounts of battles won and lost, strategy and tactics, the roles played by heaven and earth. The problem he had set me was how to take the town of Yamagata. It had been a theoretical problem, no more; Yamagata was still under the control of Arai through his interim governor, though there had been reports that the Otori planned to retake their former city and were assembling an army on their southern border near Tsuwano. Matsuda had intended to approach Arai on my behalf and make peace between us, whereupon I would serve Arai while pursuing the Otori inheritance. However, I was now acutely aware that if I risked inciting Arai's enmity anew by marrying Kaede I might very well need to take Yamagata at once. It added a certain sense of reality to my studies of strategy.

I knew the town so well: I'd explored every street; I'd climbed into the castle. And I knew the terrain around it, its mountains, valleys, hills, and rivers. My main difficulty was having so few men at my command, a thousand at most. Yamagata was a prosperous town, but the winter had been hard on everyone. If I attacked in early spring, could the castle withstand a long siege? Would diplomacy bring about a surrender where force would not? What advantages did I have over the defenders?

While I was brooding over these problems, my thoughts turned to the outcast, Jo-An. I had said I would send for him in the spring, but I was still not sure I wanted to. I could never forget the hungry, passionate look in his eyes, in the eyes of the boatman and the other outcasts. "He's your man now," Jo-An had said of the boatman. "We all are." Could I add outcasts to my army, or the farmers who came daily to pray and make offerings at Shigeru's grave? I had no doubt that I could count on these men if I wanted them. But was this what the warrior class did? I had never read of battles where farmers fought. Usually they stayed well clear of the combat, hating both sides equally and afterward stripping the dead impartially.

As it often did, the face of the farmer I had murdered in his secret field in the hills behind Matsue floated before my mind's eye. I heard his voice call again, "Lord Shigeru!" As much as anything else, I wanted to lay his ghost to rest. But he also brought into my mind the courage and determination of his fellows, resources that at the moment were wasted. If I used them, would he stop haunting me?

The farmers in the Otori lands, both in the existing ones around Hagi and those that had been ceded to the Tohan—Yamagata included—had loved Shigeru. They had already risen in fury after his death. I believed they would also support me, but I feared using them would weaken the loyalty of my warriors.

Back to the theoretical problem of Yamagata: If I could get rid of the interim lieutenant Arai had placed in the castle, there was a much greater chance of the city surrendering without a long siege. What I needed was an assassin I could trust. The Tribe had admitted I was the only person who could have climbed alone into Yamagata Castle, but it did not seem like a good scheme for the commander-in-chief to undertake. My thoughts began to drift a little, reminding me I'd hardly slept the night before. I wondered if I could train young boys and girls in the way the Tribe trained them. They might not have innate skills, but there was much that was simply a matter of teaching. I could see all the advantages of a network of spies.

Might there not be some disaffected Tribe members who could be persuaded to serve me? I put the thought away for the time being, but it was to return to me later.

As the day warmed up, time slowed even more. Flies, having woken from their winter sleep, were buzzing against the screens. I heard the first bush warbler calling from the forest, the glide of the swallows' wings and the snap of their beaks as they took insects. The sounds of the temple murmured around me: the tread of feet, the swish of robes, the rise and fall of chanting, the sudden clear note of a bell.

A light breeze was blowing from the south, full of the fragrance of spring. Within a week Kaede and I would be married. Life seemed to rise around me, embracing me with its vigor and energy. Yet, I was kneeling here, rapt in the study of war.

And when Kaede and I met that evening, we did not talk of love but of strategy. We had no need to talk of love; we were to be married, we were to become husband and wife. But if we were to live long enough to have children, we needed to act swiftly to consolidate our power.

I had been right in my instinct, when Makoto first told me that she was raising an army, that Kaede would make a formidable ally. She agreed with me that we should go straight to Maruyama; she told me of her meeting with Sugita Haruki in the autumn. He was waiting to hear from her, and she suggested sending some of her men to the domain to let him know of our intentions. I agreed, and thought the younger of the Miyoshi brothers, Gemba, might go with them. We sent no messages to Inuyama: The less Arai knew of our plans, the better.

"Shizuka said our marriage will enrage him," Kaede said.

I knew it probably would. We should have known better. We should have been patient. Perhaps if we had approached Arai through the proper channels, through Gemba and Kahei's aunt or through Matsuda or Sugita, he would have decided in our favor. But we were both seized by a desperate sense of urgency, knowing how short our lives might be. And so we were married a few days later, before the shrine, in the shadow of the trees that surrounded Shigeru's grave, in accordance with his will but in defiance of all the rules of our class. I suppose I might say in our defense that neither of us had had a typical upbringing. We had both escaped, for different reasons, the rigid training in obedience of most warriors' children. It gave us freedom to act as we pleased, but the elders of our class were to make us pay for it.

The weather continued warm under the south wind. On our wedding day the cherry blossoms were fully open, a mass of pink and white. Kaede's men had now been allowed to join mine and the highest-ranking warrior among them, Amano Tenzo, spoke for her and on behalf of the Shirakawa clan. When Kaede was led forward by the shrine maiden, in the red and white robes Manami had somehow managed to find for her, she looked beautiful in a timeless way, as if she were a sacred being. I spoke my name as Otori Takeo and named Shigeru and the Otori clan as my ancestors. We exchanged the ritual cups of wine, three times thrice, and as the sacred branches were offered, a sudden gust of wind sent a snow-storm of petals down on us.

It might have seemed a chilly omen, but that night after the feasting and the celebrations, when we were finally alone together, we had no thoughts of omens. In Inuyama we had made love in a sort of wild desperation, expecting to die before morning. But now, in the safety of Terayama, we had time to explore each other's body, to give and take pleasure slowly. And besides, since then Yuki had taught me something of the art of love.

We talked about our lives since we had been separated, especially about the child. We thought about its soul, launched again into the cycle of birth and death, and prayed for it. I told Kaede about my visit to Hagi and my flight through the snow. I did not tell her about Yuki, and she kept secrets from me, for though she told me a little about Lord Fujiwara, she did not go into details as to the pact they had made. I knew he had given her large amounts of money and food, and it worried me, for it made me think his views on the marriage were more fixed than hers. I felt a slight chill in my spine that may have been a premonition, but I put the thought away, for I wanted nothing to spoil my joy.

I woke toward dawn to find her sleeping in my arms. Her skin was white, silky to my touch, both warm and cool at the same time. Her hair, so long and thick it covered us both like a shawl, smelled of jasmine. I had thought her like the flower on the high mountain, completely beyond my reach, but she was here, she was mine. The world stood still in the silent night as the realization sank in. The backs of my eyes stung as tears came. Heaven was benign. The gods loved me. They had given me Kaede.

For a few days heaven continued to smile on us, giving us

gentle spring weather, every day sunny. Everyone at the temple seemed happy for us—from Manami, who beamed with delight when she brought us tea the first morning, to the abbot, who resumed my lessons, teasing me unmercifully if he caught me yawning. Scores of people made the climb up the mountain to bring gifts and wish us well, just as the village people would have done in Mino.

Only Makoto sounded a different note. "Make the most of your happiness," he said to me. "I am happy for you, believe me, but I fear it will not last."

I already knew this: I had learned it from Shigeru. "Death comes suddenly and life is fragile and brief," he had told me the day after he had saved my life in Mino. "No one can alter this either by prayers or spells." It was the fragility of life that made it so precious. Our happiness was all the more intense for our awareness of how fleeting it might be.

The cherry blossoms were already falling, the days lengthening as the season turned. The winter of preparation was over: Spring was giving way to summer, and summer was the season of war. Five battles lay ahead of us, four to win and one to lose.

ACKNOWLEDGMENTS

I would like to thank the Asialink Foundation and all my friends in Japan and Australia who have helped me in researching and writing Tales of the Otori.

In *Grass for His Pillow* I particularly want to thank Ms. Sugiyama Kazuko for her calligraphy and Simon Higgins for his advice on martial arts.

Turn the page for a preview of

Brilliance of the Moon

BATTLE FOR MARUYAMA

· 1 ·

The feather lay in my palm. I held it carefully, aware of its age and its fragility. Yet its whiteness was still translucent, the vermilion tips of the pinions still brilliant.

"It came from a sacred bird, the *houou*," Matsuda Shingen, the abbot of the temple at Terayama, told me. "It appeared to your adopted father, Shigeru, when he was only fifteen, younger than you are now. Did he ever tell you this, Takeo?"

I shook my head. Matsuda and I were standing in his room at one end of the cloister around the main courtyard of the temple. From outside, drowning out the usual sounds of the temple, the chanting, and the bells, came the urgent noise of preparations, of many people coming and going. I could hear

Kaede, my wife, beyond the gates, talking to Amano Tenzo about the problems of keeping our army fed on the march. We were preparing to travel to Maruyama, the great domain in the West to which Kaede was the rightful heir, to claim it in her name—to fight for it if necessary. Since the end of winter, warriors had been making their way to Terayama to join me, and I now had close to a thousand men, billeted in the temple and in the surrounding villages, not counting the local farmers who also strongly supported my cause.

Amano was from Shirakawa, my wife's ancestral home, and the most trusted of her retainers, a great horseman and good with all animals. In the days that followed our marriage, Kaede and her woman, Manami, had shown considerable skill in handling and distributing food and equipment. They discussed everything with Amano and had him deliver their decisions to the men. That morning he was enumerating the oxcarts and packhorses we had at our disposal. I tried to stop listening, to concentrate on what Matsuda was telling me, but I was restless, eager to get moving.

"Be patient," Matsuda said mildly. "This will only take a minute. What do you know about the *houou*?"

I reluctantly pulled my attention back to the feather in

my palm and tried to recall what my former teacher, Ichiro, had taught me when I had been living in Lord Shigeru's house in Hagi. "It is the sacred bird of legend that appears in times of justice and peace. And it is written with the same character as the name of my clan, Otori."

"Correct," Matsuda said, smiling. "It does not often appear, justice and peace being something of a rarity in these times. But Shigeru saw it and I believe the vision inspired him in his pursuit of these virtues. I told him then that the feathers were tinged with blood, and indeed his blood, his death, still drive both you and me."

I looked more closely at the feather. It lay across the scar on my right palm where I had burned my hand a long time ago, in Mino, my birthplace, the day Shigeru had saved my life. My hand was also marked with the straight line of the Kikuta, the Tribe family to which I belonged, from which I had run away the previous winter. My inheritance, my past, and my future, all seemed to be there, held in the palm of my hand.

"Why do you show it to me now?"

"You will be leaving here soon. You have been with us all winter, studying and training to prepare yourself to fulfill Shigeru's last commands to you. I wanted you to share in his vision, to remember that his goal was justice, and yours must be, too."

"I will never forget it," I promised. I bowed reverently over the feather, holding it gently in both hands, and offered it back to the abbot. He took it, bowed over it, and replaced it in the small lacquered box from which he had taken it. I said nothing, remembering all that Shigeru had done for me, and how much I still needed to accomplish for him.

"Ichiro told me about the *houou* when he was teaching me to write my name," I said finally. "When I saw him in Hagi last year he advised me to wait for him here, but I cannot wait much longer. We must leave for Maruyama within the week." I had been worrying about my old teacher since the snows had melted, for I knew that the Otori lords, Shigeru's uncles, were trying to take possession of my house and lands in Hagi and that Ichiro continued stubbornly to resist them.

I did not know it, but Ichiro was already dead. I had the news of it the next day. I was talking with Amano in the courtyard when I heard something from far below: shouts of anger, running feet, the trampling of hooves. The sound of horses plunging up the slope was unexpected and shocking. Usually no one came to the temple at Terayama on horseback. They either walked up the steep mountain path or, if unfit or very old, were carried by sturdy porters.

A few seconds later Amano heard it, too. By then I was already running to the temple gates, calling to the guards.

Swiftly they set about closing the gates and barring them. Matsuda came hurrying across the courtyard. He was not wearing armor, but his sword was in his belt. Before we could speak to each other, a challenge came from the guardhouse.

"Who dares to ride to the temple gate? Dismount and approach this place of peace with respect!"

It was Kubo Makoto's voice. One of Terayama's young warrior monks, he had become, over the last few months, my closest friend. I ran to the wooden stockade and climbed the ladder to the guardhouse. Makoto gestured toward the spy hole. Through the chinks in the wood I could see four horsemen. They had been galloping up the hill; now they pulled their heaving, snorting mounts to a halt. They were fully armed, but the Otori crest was clearly visible on their helmets. For a moment I thought that they might be messengers from Ichiro. Then my eyes fell on the basket tied to the bow of one of the saddles. My heart turned to stone. I could guess, only too easily, what was inside such a container.

The horses were rearing and cavorting, not only from the exertion of the gallop, but also from alarm. Two of them were already bleeding from wounds to their hindquarters. A mob of angry men poured from the narrow path, armed with staves and sickles. I recognized some of them: They were farmers from the nearest village. The warrior at the rear made a rush at them, sword flailing, and they fell back slightly but did not disperse, maintaining their threatening stance in a tight half circle.

The leader of the horsemen flung a look of contempt at them and then called toward the gate in a loud voice.

"I am Fuwa Dosan of the Otori clan from Hagi. I bring a message from my lords Shoichi and Masahiro for the upstart who calls himself Otori Takeo."

Makoto called back, "If you are peaceful messengers, dismount and leave your swords. The gates will be opened."

I already knew what their message would be. I could feel blind fury building up behind my eyes.

"There's no need for that," Fuwa replied scornfully. "Our message is short. Tell the so-called Takeo that the Otori do not recognize his claims and that this is how they will deal with him and any who follow him."

The man alongside him dropped the reins on his horse's neck and opened the container. From it he took what I dreaded to see. Holding it by its topknot, he swung his arm and threw Ichiro's head over the wall into the temple grounds.

It fell with a slight thud onto the petaled grass of the garden.

I drew my sword, Jato, from my belt.

"Open the gate!" I shouted. "I am going out to them."

I leaped down the steps, Makoto behind me.

As the gates opened, the Otori warriors turned their horses and drove them at the wall of men around them, swords sweeping. I imagine they thought the farmers would not dare attack them. Even I was astonished at what happened next. Instead of parting to let them through, the men on foot hurled themselves at the horses. Two of the farmers died immediately, cut in half by the warriors' swords, but then the first horse came down, and its rider fell into the pack around him. The others met a similar fate. They had no chance to use their swordsmanship: They were dragged from their horses and beaten to death like dogs.

Makoto and I tried to restrain the farmers and eventually managed to drive them back from the bodies. We restored calm only by severing the warriors' heads and having them displayed on the temple gates. The unruly army threw insults at them for a while and then retired down the hill, promising in loud voices that if any other strangers dared approach the temple and insult Lord Otori Takeo, the Angel of Yamagata, they would be dealt with in the same way.

Makoto was shaking with rage—and some other emotion that he wanted to talk to me about—but I did not have the time then. I went back inside the walls. Kaede had brought white cloths and water in a wooden bowl. She was kneeling on the ground beneath the cherry trees, calmly washing the head. Its skin was blue-gray, the eyes half-closed, the neck not severed cleanly but hacked with several blows. Yet, she handled it gently, with loving care, as if it were a precious and beautiful object.

I knelt beside her, put out my hand, and touched the hair. It was streaked with gray, but the face in death looked younger than when I had last seen it, when Ichiro was alive in the house in Hagi, grieving and haunted by ghosts yet still willing to show me affection and guidance.

"Who is it?" Kaede said in a low voice.

"Ichiro. He was my teacher in Hagi. Shigeru's too."

My heart was too full to say more. I blinked away my tears. The memory of our last meeting rose in my mind. I wished I had said more to him, told him of my gratitude and my respect. I wondered how he had died, if his death had been humiliating and agonizing. I longed for the dead eyes to open, the bloodless lips to speak. How irretrievable the dead are, how completely they go from us! Even when their spirits return, they do not speak of their own deaths.

I was born and raised among the Hidden, who believe that only those who follow the commandments of the Secret God will meet again in the afterlife. Everyone else will be consumed in the fires of hell. I did not know if my adopted father Shigeru had been a believer, but he was familiar with all the teachings of the Hidden and spoke their prayers at the moment of his death, along with the name of the Enlightened One. Ichiro, his adviser and the steward of his household, had never given any such sign— in fact, rather the opposite: Ichiro had suspected from the start that Shigeru had rescued me from the warlord Iida Sadamu's persecution of the Hidden, and had watched me like a cormorant for anything that might give me away.

But I no longer followed the teachings of my childhood,

and I could not believe that a man of Ichiro's integrity and loyalty was in hell. Far stronger was my outrage at the injustice of this murder and my realization that I now had another death to avenge.

"They paid for it with their lives," Kaede said. "Why kill an old man and go to all that trouble to bring his head to you?" She washed away the last traces of blood and wrapped a clean white cloth around the head.

"I imagine the Otori lords want to draw me out," I replied. "They would prefer not to attack Terayama; they will run into Arai's soldiers if they do. They must hope to entice me over the border and meet me there." I longed for such a meeting, to punish them once and for all. The warriors' deaths had temporarily assuaged my fury, but I could feel it simmering in my heart. However, I had to be patient; my strategy was first to withdraw to Maruyama and build up my forces there. I would not be dissuaded from that.

I touched my brow to the grass, bidding my teacher good-bye. Manami came from the guest rooms and knelt a little way behind us.

"I've brought the box, lady," she whispered.

"Give it to me," Kaede replied. It was a small container

woven from willow twigs and strips of red-dyed leather. She took it and opened it. The smell of aloes rose from it. She put the white wrapped bundle inside and arranged the aloes round it. Then she placed the box on the ground in front of her, and the three of us bowed again before it.

A bush warbler called its spring song and a cuckoo responded from deep in the forest, the first I had heard that year.

We held the funeral rites the following day and buried the head next to Shigeru's grave. I made arrangements for another stone to be erected for Ichiro. I longed to know what had happened to the old woman, Chiyo, and the rest of the household at Hagi. I was tormented by the thought that the house no longer existed, that it would have been burned: the tea room, the upper room where we had so often sat looking out onto the garden, the nightingale floor, all destroyed, their song silenced forever. I wanted to rush to Hagi to claim my inheritance before it was taken from me. But I knew this was exactly what the Otori hoped I would do.

Five farmers died outright and two died later from their wounds. We buried them in the temple graveyard. Two of the horses were badly hurt, and Amano had them killed mercifully, but the other two were unharmed; one I liked in particular, a handsome black stallion that reminded me of Shigeru's horse, Kyu, and could have been its half brother. At Makoto's insistence we buried the Otori warriors with full rites, too, praying that their ghosts, outraged at their ignoble deaths, would not linger to haunt us.

That evening the abbot came to the guest room and we talked until late into the night. Makoto and Miyoshi Kahei, one of my allies and friends from Hagi, were also with us; Kahei's younger brother Gemba had been sent to Maruyama to tell the domain's senior retainer, Sugita Haruki, of our imminent departure. Sugita had assured Kaede the previous winter of his support for her claim. Kaede did not stay with us—for various reasons, she and Makoto were not at ease in each other's presence and she avoided him as much as possible—but I told her beforehand to sit behind the screen so she could hear what was said. I wanted to know her opinion afterward. In the short time since our marriage I had come to talk to her as I had never talked to anyone in my life. I had been silent for so long, it seemed now I could not get enough of sharing my thoughts with her. I relied on her judgment and her wisdom.

"So now you are at war," the abbot said, "and your army has had its first skirmish."

"Hardly an army," Makoto said. "A rabble of farmers! How are you going to punish them?"

"What do you mean?" I replied.

"Farmers are not supposed to kill warriors," he said. "Anyone else in your situation would punish them with the utmost cruelty. They would be crucified, boiled in oil, flayed alive."

"They will be if the Otori get hold of them," Kahei muttered.

"They were fighting on my behalf," I said. Privately, I thought the warriors had deserved their shameful end, though I was sorry I had not killed them all myself. "I'm not going to punish them. I'm more concerned with how to protect them."

"You have let an ogre out," Makoto said. "Let's hope you can contain it."

The abbot smiled into his wine cup. Quite apart from his earlier comments on justice, he had been teaching me strategy all winter and, having heard my theories on the capture of Yamagata and other campaigns, knew how I felt about my farmers.

"The Otori seek to draw me out," I said to him, as I had said earlier to Kaede.

"Yes, you must resist the temptation," he replied. "Naturally your first instinct is for revenge, but even if you defeated their army in a confrontation, they would simply retreat to Hagi. A long siege would be a disaster. The city is virtually impregnable, and sooner or later you would have to deal with Arai's forces at your rear."

Arai Daiichi was the warlord from Kumamoto who had taken advantage of the overthrow of the Tohan to seize control of the Three Countries. I had enraged him by disappearing with the Tribe the previous year, and now my marriage to Kaede would certainly enrage him further. He had a huge army, and I did not want to be confronted by it before I had strengthened my own.

"Then we must go first to Maruyama, as planned. But if I leave the temple unprotected, you and the people of the district may be punished by the Otori."

"We can bring many people within the walls," the abbot said. "I think we have enough arms and supplies to hold the Otori off if they do attack. Personally, I don't think they will. Arai and his allies will not relinquish Yamagata without a long struggle, and many among the Otori would be reluctant to destroy this place, which is sacred to the clan. Anyway they will be more concerned with pursuing you." He paused and then went on: "You can't fight a war without being prepared for sacrifice. Men will die in the battles you fight, and if you lose, many of them, including you yourself, may be put to death very painfully. The Otori do not recognize your adoption: They do not know your ancestry; as far as they are concerned you are an upstart, not one of their class. You cannot hold back from action because people will die as a result. Even your farmers know that. Seven of them died today, but those who survived are not sad. They are celebrating their victory over those who insulted you."

"I know that," I said, glancing at Makoto. His lips were pressed together tightly, and though his face showed no other expression, I felt his disapproval. I was aware yet again of my weaknesses as a commander. I was afraid both Makoto and Kahei, brought up in the warrior tradition, would come to despise me.

"We joined you by our own choice, Takeo," the abbot went on, "because of our loyalty to Shigeru and because we believe your cause is just."

I bowed my head, accepting the rebuke and vowing he would never have to speak to me in that vein again. "We will leave for Maruyama the day after tomorrow."

"Makoto will go with you," the abbot said. "As you know, he has made your cause his own."

Makoto's lips curved slightly as he nodded in agreement.

Later that night, around the second half of the hour of the Rat, when I was about to lie down beside Kaede, I heard voices outside, and a few moments later Manami called quietly to us to say that a monk had come with a message from the guardhouse.

"We have taken a prisoner," he said when I went to speak to him. "He was spotted skulking in the bushes beyond the gate. The guards pursued him and would have killed him on the spot, but he called your name and said he was your man."

"I'll come and talk to him," I said, taking up Jato, suspecting it could only be the outcast Jo-An. Jo-An had seen me at Yamagata when I had released his brother and other members of the Hidden into death. It was he who had given me the name of the Angel of Yamagata. Then he had saved my life on my desperate journey to Terayama in the winter. I had told him I would send for him in the spring and that he should wait until he heard from me, but he acted in unpredictable ways, usually in response to what he claimed was the voice of the Secret God.

It was a soft, warm night, the air already holding summer's humidity. In the cedars an owl was hooting. Jo-An lay on the ground just inside the gate. He'd been trussed up roughly: His legs were bent under him, his hands bound behind his back. His face was streaked with dirt and blood, his hair matted. He was moving his lips very slightly, praying soundlessly. Two monks were watching him from a careful distance, their faces twisted in contempt.

I called his name and his eyes opened. I saw relief shine in them. He tried to scrabble into a kneeling position and fell forward, unable to save himself with his hands. His face hit the dirt.

"Untie him," I said.

One of the monks said, "He is an outcast. We should not touch him."

"Who tied him up?"

"We did not realize then," the other said.

"You can cleanse yourselves later. This man saved my life. Untie him."

Reluctantly they went to Jo-An, lifted him up, and loosened the cords that bound him. He crawled forward and prostrated himself at my feet.

"Sit up, Jo-An," I said. "Why are you here? I said you were to come when I sent for you. You were lucky not to be killed, turning up here without warning, without permission."

The last time I'd seen him I'd been almost as shabbily dressed as he was, a fugitive, exhausted and starving. Now I was aware of the robe I wore, my hair dressed in the warrior style, the sword in my belt. I knew the sight of me talking to the outcast would shock the monks profoundly. Part of me was tempted to have him thrown out, to deny that there was any relationship between us, and to throw him from my life at the same time. If I so ordered the guards, they would kill him immediately with no second thought. Yet, I could not do it. He had saved my life; moreover, for the sake of the bond between us, both born into the Hidden, I had to treat him not as an outcast but as a man.

"No one will kill me until the Secret One calls me home," he muttered, raising his eyes and looking at me.

"Until that time, my life is yours." There was little light where we stood, just the lamp the monk had brought from the guardhouse and placed on the ground near us, but I could see Jo-An's eyes burning. I wondered, as I often had before, if he were not alive at all but a visitant from another world.

"What do you want?" I said.

"I have something to tell you. Very important. You'll be glad I came."

The monks had stepped back out of pollution's way but were still close enough to hear us.

"I need to talk to this man," I said. "Where should we go?"

They threw an anguished look at each other and the older man suggested, "Maybe the pavilion, in the garden?"

"You don't need to come with me."

"We should guard Lord Otori," the younger said.

"I'm in no danger from this man. Leave us alone. But tell Manami to bring water, some food, and tea."

They bowed and left. As they crossed the courtyard they started whispering to each other. I could hear every word. I sighed.

"Come with me," I said to Jo-An. He limped after me to the pavilion, which stood in the garden not far from the large pool. Its surface glittered in the starlight, and every now and then a fish leaped from the water, flopping back with a loud splash. Beyond the pool the grayish white stones of the graves loomed out of the darkness. The owl hooted again, closer this time.

"God told me to come to you," he said when we were settled on the wooden floor of the pavilion.

"You should not talk so openly of God," I chided him. "You are in a temple. The monks have no more love for the Hidden than the warriors."

"You are here," he muttered. "You are our hope and our protection."

"I'm just one person. I can't protect all of you from the way a whole country feels."

He was silent for a moment or two. Then he said, "The Secret One thinks about you all the time, even if you have forgotten him."

I did not want to listen to this sort of message.

"What do you have to tell me?" I said impatiently.

"The men you saw last year, the charcoal burners, were taking their god back to the mountain. I met them on the path. They told me the Otori armies are out, watching every road around Terayama and Yamagata. I went to look for myself. There are soldiers hidden everywhere. They will ambush you as soon as you leave. If you want to get out, you will have to fight your way through them."

His eyes were fixed on me, watching my reaction. I was cursing myself for having stayed so long at the temple. I'd been aware all along that speed and surprise were my main weapons. I should have left days before. I had been putting off leaving, waiting for Ichiro. Before my marriage I'd gone out night after night to check the roads around the temple for just such an eventuality. But since Kaede had joined me I could not tear myself away from her. Now I was trapped by my own vacillation and lack of vigilance.

"How many men would you say?"

"Five or six thousand," he replied.

I had barely a thousand.

"So you'll have to go over the mountain as you did in the winter. There's a track that goes west. No one's watching it, because there's still snow on the pass."

My mind was racing. I knew the path he meant. It went past the shrine where Makoto had planned to spend the winter before I stumbled in out of the snow on my flight to Terayama.

I'd explored it myself a few weeks earlier, turning back when the snow became too deep to wade through. I thought of my forces, men, horses, oxen: Oxen would never make it, but men and horses might. I would send them at night if possible, so the Otori would think we were still in the temple.... I would have to start at once, consult the abbot immediately.

My thoughts were interrupted by Manami and one of the manservants. The man was carrying a bowl of water. Marami brought a tray with a bowl of rice and vegetables and two cups of twig tea. She set the tray down on the floor, gazing at Jo-An with as much revulsion as if he were a viper. The man's reaction was equally horrified. I wondered briefly whether it would harm me to be seen associating with outcasts. I told them to leave us and they did so quickly, though I could hear Manami's disapproving muttering all the way back to the guesthouse.

Jo-An washed his hands and face, then joined his hands together to say the first prayer of the Hidden. Even as I found myself responding to the familiar words, a wave of irritation swept over me. He had risked his own life again to bring me this vital news, but I wished he showed more discretion, and my spirits sank at the thought of the liability he might become.

When he had finished eating I said, "You'd better leave. You have a long journey home."

He made no response, but sat, head turned slightly sideways, in the listening position I was by now familiar with.

"No," he said finally. "I am to go with you."

"It's impossible. I don't want you with me."

"God wants it," he said.

There was nothing I could do to argue him out of it, short of killing him or imprisoning him, and these seemed shabby rewards for his help to me.

"Very well," I said, "but you can't stay in the temple."

"No," he agreed docilely, "I have to fetch the others."

"What others, Jo-An?"

"The rest of us. The ones who came with me. You saw some of them."

I had seen these men at the tannery by the river where Jo-An worked, and I would never forget the way they had stared after me with burning eyes. I knew they looked to me for justice and protection. I remembered the feather: Justice was what Shigeru had desired. I also had to pursue it for the sake of his memory and for these living men.

Jo-An put his hands together again and gave thanks for the food.

A fish leaped in the silence.

"How many are there?" I asked.

"About thirty. They're hiding in the mountains. They've been crossing the border in ones and twos for the last weeks."

"Isn't the border guarded?"

"There've been skirmishes between the Otori and Arai's men. At the moment there's a standoff. The borders are all open. The Otori have made it clear they're not challenging Arai or hoping to retake Yamagata. They only want to eliminate you."

It seemed to be everyone's mission.

"Do the people support them?" I asked.

"Of course not!" he said almost impatiently. "You know who they support: the Angel of Yamagata. So do we all. Why else are we here?"

I was not sure I wanted their support, but I could not help but be impressed by their courage.

"Thank you," I said.

He grinned then, showing his missing teeth, reminding me of the torture he had already suffered because of me.

"We'll meet you on the other side of the mountain. You'll need us then, you'll see."

I had the guards open the gates and said good-bye to him. I watched his slight, twisted shape as he scuttled away into the darkness. From the forest a vixen screamed, a sound like a ghost in torment. I shivered. Jo-An seemed guided and sustained by some great supernatural power. Though I no longer believed in it, I feared its force like a superstitious child.

I went back to the guesthouse, my skin crawling. I removed my clothes and, despite the lateness of the hour, told Manami to take them away, wash and purify them, and then come to the bathhouse. She scrubbed me all over and I soaked in the hot water for ten or fifteen minutes. Putting on fresh clothes, I sent the servant to fetch Kahei and then to ask the abbot if we might speak with him. It was the first half of the hour of the Ox.

I met Kahei in the passageway, told him briefly what had transpired, and went with him to the abbot's room, sending the servant to fetch Makoto from the temple, where he was keeping the night vigil. We came to the decision that we would move the entire army as soon as possible, apart from a small band of horsemen who would remain at Terayama for a day to fight as a rear guard.

Kahei and Makoto went immediately to the village beyond the gates to rouse Amano and the other men and start packing up food and equipment. The abbot ordered servants to inform the monks, reluctant to sound the temple bell at this hour of night in case we sent a warning to spies. I went to Kaede.

She was waiting for me, already in her sleeping robe, her hair loose down her back like a second robe, intensely black against the ivory material and her white skin. The sight of her, as always, took my breath away. Whatever happened to us, I would never forget this springtime we had had together. My life seemed full of undeserved blessings, but this was the greatest of them.

"Manami said an outcast came and you let him in and spoke with him." Her voice was as shocked as her woman's had been.

"Yes, he's called Jo-An. I met him in Yamagata." I undressed, put on my robe, and sat opposite her, knee to knee.

Her eyes searched my face. "You look exhausted. Come and lie down."

"I will; we must try and sleep for a few hours. We march at first light. The Otori have surrounded the temple; we are going over the mountain."